This Family Is Driving Me Crazy

This Family Is Driving Me Crazy

TEN STORIES ABOUT SURVIVING YOUR FAMILY

EDITED BY

M. Jerry Weiss and Helen S. Weiss

G. P. PUTNAM'S SONS • PENGUIN YOUNG READERS GROUP

G. P. PUTNAM'S SONS • A division of Penguin Young Readers Group. Published by The Penguin Group. Penguin Group (USA) Inc., 375 Hudson Street, New York, NY 10014, U.S.A. Penguin Group (Canada), 90 Eglinton Avenue East, Suite 700, Toronto, Ontario M4P 2Y3, Canada (a division of Pearson Penguin Canada Inc.). Penguin Books Ltd, 80 Strand, London WC2R 0RL, England. Penguin Ireland, 25 St. Stephen's Green, Dublin 2, Ireland (a division of Penguin Books Ltd.). Penguin Group (Australia), 250 Camberwell Road, Camberwell, Victoria 3124, Australia (a division of Pearson Australia Group Pty Ltd). Penguin Books India Pvt Ltd, 11 Community Centre, Panchsheel Park, New Delhi— 110 017, India. Penguin Group (NZ), 67 Apollo Drive, Rosedale, North Shore 0632, New Zealand (a division of Pearson New Zealand Ltd). Penguin Books (South Africa) (Pty) Ltd, 24 Sturdee Avenue, Rosebank, Johannesburg 2196, South Africa. Penguin Books Ltd, Registered Offices: 80 Strand, London WC2R 0RL, England.

Design by Richard Amari.
Text set in Life Roman.

Library of Congress Cataloging-in-Publication Data
This family is driving me crazy : ten stories about surviving your family/edited by M. Jerry Weiss and Helen S. Weiss. v. cm. Contents: Wimp of Sparta/Gordon Korman—Orway otnay otay eBay?/David Lubar—American teen/Mel Glenn—The most mauve there is/ Nancy Springer—Tunnel vision/John Ritter—For the love of pork/Jack Gantos—Another chance/Sharon Dennis Wyeth—Happily (sorta) ever after (maybe)/Dian Curtis Regan— Listen/Joan Bauer—Midnight bus to Georgia/Walter Dean Myers. 1. Young adult fiction, American. 2. Family life—Juvenile fiction. [1. Short stories. 2. Family life—Fiction.] I. Weiss, M. Jerry (Morton Jerry), 1926– II. Weiss, Helen S. PZ5.T315 2009 [Fic]—dc22
2009006821
ISBN 978-0-399-25040-8
1 3 5 7 9 10 8 6 4 2

To Bob Small and Paul and Carole Hirth

Contents

Foreword

Families can drive you crazy! The complex nature of family dynamics creates an excellent variety of experiences and emotions. Sometimes there is tension and pain. Often there is love and compassion.

We hope that the short stories and poems in this collection might give you some insight into your own problems. It is reassuring to realize you're not the only one going through this.

The ten talented authors who contributed to this anthology offer a mix of memorable and diverse characters. Sometimes they are funny; sometimes they are sad. Humor and pathos can intermingle. But family conflict is at the heart of each story. And in the end, each shows proof that while our families do drive us crazy, we love them anyway.

We thank the authors who contributed to this book. They are a most wonderful group who developed the theme through their creative talents.

We express our deepest gratitude to Timothy Travaglini, our patient and encouraging editor.

Helen and Jerry

This Family Is Driving Me Crazy

Wimp of Sparta

By

Gordon Korman

Top Chef was on in the hotel room when I got the call about the shark attack.

My mother's voice betrayed no panic on the phone. "He's at Mercy Hospital."

I didn't panic either. In the Sparta family, the trip to the hospital was as much a part of going on vacation as airport security and hotel food.

"Dad or Tyson?" Tyson—my fifteen-year-old brother. Born without fear. Or brains.

"Both."

This was a wrinkle. "Both?"

"Tyson's not serious. He just hit his head on the side of the boat when they hauled up what was left of the shark cage. I swear—we should sue the whole crew! To abort our dive because of one little great white—"

That got my attention. "Dad was attacked by a great white?"

"Don't be so dramatic, Peter," she admonished me. "The doctors say it's a dermal abrasion from the sharkskin."

"Where's Kelly?" I asked. She was the oldest. Seventeen, and possibly crazier than Tyson.

"Giving blood," Mom replied. "Dad has a rare type. They don't have much O-neg in this corner of Australia."

"He needs a transfusion for a scratch?"

She was impatient. "There are scratches, and there are scratches. You know how sharks can be when there's blood in the water."

So now it wasn't just the crew who overreacted. It was the great white, too.

"I have to hang up, Peter," she said suddenly. "They're wheeling your father out of Emergency. Take a taxi to the hospital. And don't forget to ask the driver for a receipt."

Welcome to the world of Sparta family vacations. The Spartans, Dad called us. He always compared us to the ancient Greeks. Personally, I didn't see the connection. Those legendary warriors fought battles for the protection of their homes and loved ones, the survival of their city-state. But Dad wasn't protecting his family when he jumped in the water with that great white. On the contrary, he practically got them all killed.

When we traveled, there was no Disney World in the itinerary, no Waikiki. Sun and sand meant crossing the Gobi desert on camelback. The closest we got to a water park was our raft trip down the cataracts of the Nile, complete with belligerent hippos and eighteen-foot crocs.

Daredevils, thrill seekers, or just plain nuts—the Spartans had been called all those, and a whole lot more. If you look up *maniac* in the dictionary, you'll probably find a family portrait. But I wouldn't be in it.

I didn't hang from sky hooks or fly through the air with the greatest of ease. Somehow the daredevil gene missed me; I got the cowardly recessive. I was the one who sat in the hotel waiting for the phone to ring with directions to the hospital. My biggest responsibility was to remember the taxi receipt. Believe it or not, near-death experiences were tax deductible. Since Dad wrote articles about the family adventures, my cab rides to the hospital were legitimate business expenses. So were doctor bills, rehab, crutches, neck braces, various creams and liniments, even Advil—and we went through piles of that.

"You can't live your life cocooned in Bubble Wrap," my father lectured me time and time again. "The world is full of rich and glorious experience, and you're missing it!"

A lot of that rich and glorious experience had to do with doctors and hospitals. In his forty-seven years, Calvin Sparta had broken thirty-two bones, not to mention his three concussions and one fractured skull. His wife, my mother, left her eyebrows at four thousand feet over the Bermuda Triangle while adjusting the flame of a hot air balloon. Kelly and Tyson already bore the scars of battle as well. Both were convinced I'd been switched at birth with their real brother. Somewhere out there was a true biological Spartan, wondering why his parents wouldn't let him BASE jump off the Empire State Building.

But they had a point. Why was I such a misfit? Not that I yearned to be part of their kamikaze lifestyle, but—well, why didn't I? It was like coming from a long line of concert pianists, and you were all thumbs. Even if you had no interest in music, it still hurt to be left out.

I didn't belong. I didn't *want* to belong their way. Still, I wanted to belong *some* way. I kept on hoping that there would turn out to be an alternate path to full membership in the Sparta clan—one that didn't come at the end of a bungee cord, approaching terminal velocity.

Keep dreaming.

I had traveled the world with nothing to show for it but frequent-flyer miles. I never did anything. I never saw anything that didn't happen to be along the road between our hotel and the hospital. My role was to wait for the damage report. And it always came. Broken jaw, ruptured spleen, three-point landing on knees and nose, dislocated shoulder, missing teeth. I endured my parents' lectures about living life to the fullest and my siblings' taunts about what a wimp I was.

Deep down, I knew I was the most courageous of all. It took a lot of guts to sit by the phone for the call that would one day surely come—the call that wouldn't be about scrapes and bruises, or even fractures. The one where the directions wouldn't be to any hospital, but to the local morgue.

Dad was in somewhat better shape when I joined the family at Mercy Hospital that day. His chest and arm were wrapped mummy-style in white bandages, but he was sitting up in bed, and his energy level was high as he argued with the doctor.

"Of course we're going back out on the reef—as soon as I find a boat captain who won't panic and raise the cage at the first little glitch!"

"The door falling off a shark cage isn't a 'little glitch,'" the doctor said soothingly. "And the poor man probably didn't expect you to jump out of it."

"I hadn't taken any pictures!" Dad roared, as if this explained everything. He picked up the phone on the bedside table. "I hope it isn't too late to book another charter for tomorrow morning."

The doctor took the receiver from Dad's hand and returned it to its cradle. "You've had forty percent of the skin scraped off your torso and upper arm. You put a wound like that in the ocean, you'll attract every shark this side of the Horn of Africa. I'm afraid you're high and dry, my American friend."

I found a rare unbandaged spot on my father's shoulder and patted it. "A little relaxation will do us good, Dad."

Tyson glared at me from beneath the dressing on his forehead. "Relaxation doesn't get your blood pumping."

"From what I hear, yours was pumping all over the Great Barrier Reef," I retorted.

"Just because we can't dive doesn't mean we can't score some adrenaline," Kelly pointed out. "We're in Australia! There's action in the Outback, right, doc?"

"I suppose," the doctor told her. "But it's a very big country. The Outback is hundreds of kilometers away. You'd have to charter a plane."

Dad sat up, suppressing a grimace as bandages tugged against shark-abraded skin. "Great idea. A plane." With a practiced motion, he tore off his hospital bracelet. "And parachutes."

What do you do if you can't dive with sharks?

If your last name is Sparta, you go skydiving.

This family was driving me crazy.

Fast-forward twenty-four hours. Streaking across the sky at 11,000 feet, I counted the chutes blooming into colorful patterns below the aircraft. Yes, I was along for the ride this time. Not to jump of course, but to "see what a rush you're missing"—Dad's words, not mine.

"The only rush I'll be missing is the ambulance ride," I had told him sourly.

Actually, no airborne jump could have made me as nauseated as the flight to the drop site. The plane was perfect for Dad's band of ancient warriors. It looked, rattled, and definitely smelled like it had seen action in the Trojan War.

Four skydivers, four parachutes. I sighed my relief into the hanging oxygen mask. The pilot flashed me a thumbs-up as he undid his seat belt to reach for a thermos of coffee.

Then it happened.

The plane gave a violent lurch. A bloody mass of feathers thumped into the front windscreen—the propeller-mangled remains of a bird. The jolt bounced the pilot clear out of his chair, slamming his head against the cockpit bulkhead. Only my seat belt kept me from a similar fate.

With no one at the controls, the nose of the plane turned downward.

"Mister!" I batted off my mask. "Captain! *Hey!*"

Sprawled in a heap on the flight deck, the pilot did not stir.

I threw off the belt and made my way forward, legs unsteady as our descent steepened. I knelt by the pilot. He was out like a light.

"Wake up!" I pleaded, slapping at his cheeks. "Come on, mister, *nobody's flying the plane!*" I uncorked the thermos and poured lukewarm coffee over his head. No response.

A funny sensation took hold in my stomach—that roller-coaster feeling of free fall. My head jerked up sharply enough to bring on whiplash. The sky had disappeared from the front windshield. In its place, the coast of Queensland, Australia, was hurtling toward me at full speed!

In a blind panic, I leaped into the pilot's seat and heaved back on the wheel, like I'd seen people do in movies. "Wake up!" I rasped over my shoulder as I pulled with all my might.

My efforts elicited no sign of life from the unconscious pilot, but slowly, a brilliant expanse of light blue swung into view. We were flying level again—the nose of the plane was just below the horizon. I checked the altimeter—2700. Was that feet or meters? Or donuts, for that matter! I couldn't even be sure this *was* the altimeter. For all I knew, it was the fuel gauge or the tire-pressure indicator or the toy from the captain's last Happy Meal!

Who was I kidding? I couldn't fly a plane. "Wake up!" I screamed yet again at the unmoving pilot. The irony of it nearly tore me in two. For twelve years, I had resisted an entire family of daredevils and maniacs, always taking the safe path. How could I have known that today the safe path would have been to jump out of the plane with the daredevils and maniacs?

I picked up the radio microphone and barked, "Mayday! Mayday!" Desperately, I twisted the dial. "Can anybody hear me? My name is Peter Sparta, and I'm in a plane with an unconscious pilot!" Nothing. "Aw, come on, *Mayday*, dammit!" Either the system was dead or I just couldn't figure out how to make it work. One way or the other, I was on my own.

My eyes filled with tears. I'd always known that, sooner or later, somebody was going to get killed on one of these Sparta misadventures. But I never imagined it would be *me*.

I set my jaw. All those taxi rides were to the hospital instead of the cemetery for a reason—Spartans were survivors. Somewhere, buried deep inside the wimp my family had driven me to become, was the inner Spartan who could land this plane.

One benefit of hundreds of hours watching TV in hotel

rooms while my family danced with death: I had a basic sense of how an airplane worked. Even this old junker was loaded with hundreds of little instruments, gauges, and other baffling doohickeys. I ignored all of them but two. The wheel moved me up, down, port, and starboard. And the throttle—the black stick beside the seat—regulated engine power.

I can do this, I told myself. *I'm a Spartan.*

Gently, I eased the wheel forward, pointing the nose of the plane downward. The roller-coaster feeling came almost immediately, and the horizon pivoted up and out of view. The altimeter dial spun in a circle as we plummeted. I thought of all the airplane landings I'd seen—the graceful descent, the delicate touchdown. No way was this the same thing. This was a suicide plunge!

Heart pounding like a jackhammer, I pulled back on the wheel. "If you're planning to wake up," I shouted at the pilot, "this would be a great time!"

He didn't stir, but amazingly, the horizon returned to the windscreen, and I was able to straighten out the plane. I checked the altimeter—900. Feet, I guessed—the ground looked about that far away. Could I land on it? How flat did terrain have to be in order to pass for a runway?

There was no way to be sure. Yet one thing was certain. I had to try.

Besides, I had bigger worries. How could I descend without putting the plane into a nosedive? Maybe I was just flying too fast. With effort, I pried my trembling right hand from the wheel and transferred it to the throttle. Breathing a silent prayer, I nudged the stick backward a fraction of an inch. The tone of the engine noise changed slightly. I felt the speed slacken a little. And something else happened— something totally unexpected.

As the aircraft slowed, the nose dipped and the plane began to move lower—not the screaming, headlong dive of a minute ago, but a smooth, gradual descent.

Cut speed, and the plane goes down on its own!

Millimeter by millimeter, I pulled back on the stick, my eyes glued to the altimeter. I'd made it all the way down to 150 feet when a tinny distorted voice was suddenly yelling at me.

"Climb to an altitude of fourteen hundred feet!"

Shocked, I glanced over at the pilot, but he was still out cold.

"This is Cairns Air Traffic Control! Identify yourself!"

The radio!

"I'm Peter Sparta!" I shouted helplessly. Terror does

strange things to you. Yes, I knew that nobody could hear me unless I picked up the microphone. But with one hand on the throttle and the other on the wheel, that wasn't an option right now.

"Repeat—climb to an altitude of fourteen hundred feet! You're too low over a populated area. . . ."

Populated area?

I looked down to see houses, streets, cars—a town! Unbelievable! In the emptiest country on earth, I had managed to run out of empty!

"Climb!" the voice on the radio practically howled.

"Okay!" I let go of the throttle and yanked on the wheel with both hands. And I did climb—for about three feet. Then the plane began to shake, lurching lower in violent spasms as the engine sputtered and choked.

I've slowed down too much to ascend!

I straightened the wheel, and the ride smoothed a little. I checked the altimeter—60 feet.

"This is Cairns Air Traffic Control calling unidentified aircraft—"

"Shut up!" Sorry, Cairns Air Traffic Control, but I wasn't about to crash and burn just because you made the mistake of assuming I knew how to fly a plane.

I was right over a wide boulevard, low enough to read brand names on billboards—*well, what do you know, they have Fruit of the Loom underwear in Australia*. A split-second decision was required, and I made it. This was going to be my landing strip. I'd just have to pray the cars would be able to get out of my way. Fifty thousand useless gadgets, but nobody thought to put a simple horn on this dumb plane. Evidently, the manufacturer must have felt that if a motorist was too clueless to notice tons of machinery screaming down on his head, a polite honk wasn't likely to capture his attention.

Okay—landing gear. I scanned the instrument panel in petrified befuddlement. How did you put down the wheels on this crate? Unless this was one of those planes with fixed landing gear—yes? No? Maybe? Furiously, I tried to conjure a picture of the plane parked on the tarmac as Dad and Tyson had loaded the parachutes and gear. For the life of me—and it was literally going to come to that—I couldn't seem to call up an angle that showed what was underneath the fuselage.

Forget it. No time. All I could do was point the nose at the center line of the road. And pray.

The altimeter was at zero—useless. I hadn't touched

down yet, but I was close—close enough to make out the cowed faces in the convertible off to my left. And that little girl—the one pointing and shrieking—were those braces on her teeth . . . ?

Now!

I yanked the throttle all the way back. With a jerk and a cough, the engine stalled and I was falling. I simultaneously screamed and wheezed, creating an instant of perfect, silent terror as the plane dropped ten feet.

Whump! The bouncing impact of inflated rubber. Tires— blessed tires! Fixed landing gear! *Thank you, God. . . .*

The wallop tossed the pilot from his resting place and sent him rolling into a bulkhead. With a painful groan, he sat up and tried to blink the cobwebs out of his eyes. "Ohhhh—what happened?"

"Never mind that!" I barked. "How do you stop this crazy thing?"

Cars spun out and drove up on the sidewalk as the runaway aircraft jounced down the road at breakneck speed.

The wildness of the situation brought him back in a hurry. "Use the brakes!"

"*What* brakes?"

"The pedals!"

I looked around frantically. There were four pedals at my feet. I picked one and stomped on it. Instead of stopping, the plane swerved sharply to the right. We jumped the curb, crashed through a line of sawhorses, caromed over an expanse of broken concrete, and rattled out onto an old abandoned pier. Weathered timbers became a gray-brown blur as we hurtled along the dock.

"Not *those* pedals!" rasped the pilot. "The upper ones!"

I stomped on the brakes and pressed down with every ounce of force left in my exhausted body. The wheels locked up, and we skidded toward the gleaming Pacific.

"Come *on!*" I grunted, bracing my back against the pilot's chair for more strength.

The end of the pier was coming up fast. I stared in horror. We weren't going to stop in time.

The nose dropped as the front wheel bounced over the edge. The ancient planks split and splintered under the impact of the belly of the plane. And then—silence.

I looked around, barely daring to breathe. We were no longer moving.

"Yes!" I cheered, leaping up, fist held high. "Spartans are survivors!"

But the weight of the aircraft was too much for the ramshackle wharf. With a groan and a crunch, the dilapidated structure fell apart, and the Pacific Ocean tilted and rose to meet me.

Mom, Dad, Kelly, and Tyson piled into a taxi and came to visit me in the hospital.

They forgot to get a receipt.

The other Spartans had come through their parachute jump without a scratch. Even I wasn't too badly off, except for a broken foot sustained kicking open the hatch of the sinking plane and splinters from crawling up what was left of the pier, dragging one concussed pilot. He was in stable condition three doors away, complaining of headaches and a mysterious coffee smell.

I think the doctors were only holding me because anyone who'd been through what I had should have been in full mental breakdown. The post–traumatic stress syndrome alone would be enough to kill a normal person.

But I wasn't a normal person. I was a Spartan, just like the rest of the family. Who would have guessed it?

Dad ruffled my hair. "I've never been as proud of you as I am right now."

Was he serious? When had he ever been proud of me?

"Why?" I asked him. "Because I survived or because I almost got killed?"

Tyson jostled my arm, aggravating one of many contusions. "Because you punched your ticket, man! That's got to feel good! I take back everything I said about the hospital giving us the wrong baby! You're one of us now."

"Peter was *always* one of us," Mom interceded gently but firmly. "What your brother means, honey, is that you don't have to hide in hotel rooms anymore. You're ready to take full part in all the family fun."

Family fun.

Still, Tyson was right about one thing: I *did* feel good. Great, in fact. Not while I was in the plane. That had been the most horrible experience of my life. But now that it was over, now that I had survived something even more dangerous than the wildest line item on Dad's résumé of the extreme, I could stand tall in the Sparta family—when I got out of this hospital bed, obviously.

And that gave me the cred I needed to make some rules.

"Listen up," I said. "Now that I'm a full-fledged member of the family, I have an announcement to make: I quit."

"But Peter—" Dad began.

"No buts. What I went through counts as a lifetime of adventure, and I'm retiring. Anyone got a problem with that?"

And how could they have, when I had just achieved the impossible? I had come closer to death than any of my relatives.

Okay, on the surface, not much had changed. I'd still be going on their family trips—and I'd still be the guy sitting in the hotel waiting for the phone call. The difference was this: I didn't have to apologize for it anymore. I had starred in their X-game and then some. So I could be comfortable in my own skin when I chose to stay on the sidelines.

Even in ancient Greece, for every bunch of Spartan warriors, there had to be one wimp, standing on the rocks, scanning the horizon for the ship bringing back the survivors.

It was my destiny to be that Spartan.

I think my family understood that. And after today, maybe they would even come to realize they liked me better that way.

I liked me better that way, too.

Orway Otnay Otay eBay?

By

David Lubar

Hurricane Stephanie gets some of the credit for giving Dad a new hobby, Mom a good reason not to kill Dad, and me a taste of true power. She ripped her way up the East Coast, staying far enough offshore to spare most of Florida, Georgia, and the rest of the South, then swung inland and hovered over New Jersey long enough to turn the Garden State into an aquatic mud park.

About midway through the storm, we lost electricity. That wasn't a big deal. Dad had about eight billion candles left over from his millennium stockpile. I wasn't paying too much attention back in 1999, but apparently everyone was afraid there'd be massive problems when the year 2000 started. No electricity. No water. No computers. No sunrise. Didn't happen. But Dad likes to be prepared. Which is why, besides the candles, we had lanterns, flashlights, a kerosene heater, a bicycle-powered generator, a case of dehydrated food, and some kind of gas thing plastered with warning labels about how it would kill all of us if we used it indoors.

So we had light. But no television. I paced around the living room, looking out the window every couple of minutes in hopes of seeing one of those orange cable TV vans or the green electric company trucks—anyone with the power to return the universe to its normal state of wired entertainment.

"Don't you have homework?" Mom asked.

"Just an English project. But it's not due for two months." Okay, it was due the beginning of November, and this was the end of September, so I guess it might not have been two whole months away. Still, I figured I'd told the truth.

"Maybe you should get started now," she said.

"I can't. I need to use the computer for research." I

guess that was pretty much true, too. Besides, I couldn't do any research until I knew my topic. Unfortunately, Ms. Cowan had told us we could write about anything we wanted. I was having a hard time narrowing down the possibilities. I'd thought about doing something on video games, but I was pretty sure that *anything you wanted* really meant *anything except what you're really interested in*.

"You don't have any other homework? Nothing at all?"

"Nothing. You don't have to look over my shoulder every day. I'm not in middle school anymore."

Mom shook her head. "You would be if I didn't keep on top of things."

"This year will be different." I didn't feel like going over the same old argument. Mom seemed to think I'd totally fail if she didn't check everything I did. More often than not, she'd stand behind me when I did my math and clear her throat if I made a mistake. Sometimes, I was surprised she didn't follow me around performing CPR just in case I forgot to breathe. Maybe I'd gotten a couple of bad grades, but I was never in serious danger of staying back.

"Well, find something to do," Mom said.

"Read a book," Dad suggested.

"I don't have anything good to read," I told him.

"I can fix that." Dad grabbed a flashlight and headed for the basement.

"Now look what you've done," Mom said as the inevitable sound of toppling boxes drifted up from below.

Dad saves stuff. He's got old clothes he'll never fit into again, magazines, postcards, junk mail, cardboard tubes, coffee cans, and the accumulated equipment from a lifetime habit of switching hobbies. Within the span of my memory, Dad has photographed birds, carved walking sticks, made fishing lures, brewed beer, collected stamps, designed stained-glass windows, played the zither, and bred Siamese fighting fish.

Unfortunately, the leftovers tend to get mixed together. Dad isn't very organized about storing things. And each search mission makes the jumble worse. Mom keeps asking him to get rid of some of it, but he's never gotten more than halfway to the garbage can without freezing, staring at whatever he's carrying, and saying, "It would be a shame to throw it out. I'm sure somebody could use it."

The big problem is that I'm usually the somebody he has in mind. He's always trying to get me interested in his latest obsession.

After about twenty minutes down below, Dad emerged

from the basement and held out a musty paperback. "Try this," he said.

"No, thanks." My teachers already fed me enough books.

"Come on. I'll make you a deal. Just read the first page. If you don't like it, I won't say another word. Okay?"

I glanced at the cover. *Harridan, Barbarian Swordsman,* by Brutus Jacobs. The guy on the cover looked like an ad for steroids. I could just imagine what would happen if you pricked him with a pin. Pop go the biceps. He had a sword in one hand and somebody's head in the other. Just the head.

"One page," Dad said. "It won't kill you."

I shrugged and took the book from him. If I read the page, he'd leave me alone. Besides, the first page didn't start at the top, so it wasn't really even a full page. It wouldn't take long. I started reading.

Three hours later, I put the book down.

"Well?" Dad asked.

"Pretty cool," I admitted. Actually, it was one of the best books I'd read in a long time. Okay—that wasn't exactly a long list. Mostly, I just read the stuff they assigned in school. This was way different. It was full of action, but it was also really funny. Harridan might spend all his time killing evil sorcerers and fighting enemy warlords, but he did it with wit and style. Sort of like James Bond in a loincloth. And the chapters had great titles, like "It Takes a Sharp Sword to Get Ahead," "Don't Make Me Axe You Again," and "How to Dis-arm Your Opponent."

"Got any more?" I asked Dad. I swear, if we read books like that in English, I'd be an A-plus student, which would get Mom off my back.

"You're in luck," he said. "Jacobs wrote at least twenty Harridan novels."

Mom groaned and mumbled something that sounded like "literary popcorn" as Dad sprang up from the couch and disappeared once again into the great subterranean crap mines.

After the usual interval filled with the muted thumps of crashing piles, Dad returned balancing a towering armful of books.

I tore into them like they were a plate of fresh-baked brownies. Or popcorn, I guess. Even after the power returned, I kept reading. I put on the TV for background noise, but I didn't put down the books.

All the Harridan novels were numbered. I decided to read them in the order they were published, which was no problem for the first six books. But, as I discovered a couple days later, number seven wasn't in the stack. According to the list I found in number eight, the missing one was *Harridan and the Dragons of Dragoff.*

"Where's number seven?" I asked Dad.

"It's not there?"

"Nope."

"I'll find it."

Dad dashed downstairs. Mom gave me an annoyed look, then asked, "Don't you have homework? It's bad enough we have a basement full of trash. I hate to see you filling your mind with it."

"No homework," I said. "And I like those books." I paced and waited.

An hour later, Dad came back up, slumped in defeat. "Maybe I loaned it to someone," he said. "Always a bad move. You never get books back. Try the bookstore."

I headed out that afternoon for Book Locker. They had the first three Harridan books on the shelves, and some of the higher numbers. But they didn't have Harridan number seven.

I checked with the girl at the register. "Do you know if you have any other Harridan novels in stock?"

She gave her gum a couple careful chews, then asked, "Who?"

"Harridan. By Brutus Jacobs."

"Did you look on the shelves?"

"Yeah."

"Well, if it's not on the shelves, I guess we don't have it."

"Can you check?"

"Uh, I guess. What was the name?"

"Harridan."

"Hold on. Darn this computer. Wait. Oops. Okay. Here we go. No books by any Harridan. We got a couple Harrisons and a Harriman. You want one of those?"

"No, *Harridan* is the title. The author is Jacobs."

"Jacobs? How do you spell that?"

"J-a-c-o-b-s, Brutus Jacobs."

"Hold on. Darn this computer. Wait. Here we go. Got it." She grinned at me in triumph. "We have *Harridan, Barbarian Swordsman,* and we have—"

"That's number one. Do you have number seven?"

"Is it on the shelves?"

"I didn't see it. Look for *Harridan and the Dragons of Dragoff.*"

"Dragoff? With a *D*?"

We went a few more rounds with no results other than a strong suspicion on my part that I was being helped by someone who read a lot less than I did. I tested my suspicion by asking if they had the new William Shakespeare novel in stock. She wasn't sure but told me, "If we had it, it would be on the shelves."

I headed across town to the used book store. They had a good assortment of fantasy paperbacks, but no sign of Harridan number seven. Then I tried the library.

The book was in the catalog, and it was supposed to be on the shelves. But I couldn't find it. Neither could the librarian. "Things disappear sometimes," she said. "People walk off with books. Especially the rarer ones."

"Rarer ones?" Oh, great. This was getting worse and worse.

"I'm pretty sure it's out of print," she said.

I went home and waited for Dad to get in from work. We completely tore apart the basement. No sign of the book. We couldn't find numbers nine or fifteen, either, but I'd seen both of those at the library. We did find a whole box of really old tennis balls, including a half dozen unopened cans. And a stack of unopened junk mail, including ads for computer software, gardening magazines, and miracle car waxes.

At one point, Mom came down to the foot of the steps, stared at us, shrieked "I give up," and went back upstairs.

As I stood amid the piles of stuff, I had an idea. "I could check the Internet," I said to Dad.

"I guess we could try that. But I'll let you drive." Dad's passion for advanced technology begins and ends with the 1959 Corvette he's restoring. He doesn't even own a cell phone. "Do you know a good place to look?"

"We should start with eBay. They auction all kinds of stuff." I'd never bought anything on it, but I liked to look at the listings for video game systems, bass guitars, and other essential possessions.

Dad smirked. "I've always thought that name sounded like pig Latin."

"What's that?" All I could picture was a hog in a toga. I didn't think that's what Dad had in mind.

"Igpay atinlay," he said, as if that would clarify the issue. "Put the first consonant at the end of the word, then add an *ay* sound. If the word starts with a vowel, just add *way* to the end. We used to speak in pig Latin all the time, back when . . ." He let it go as my eyes clouded over. "Never mind. Let's see this auction thing."

I went to my bedroom and logged on, then pulled up

a web auction page and typed *Harridan* in the search window.

A message came up saying there were 837 matching items. The first page was a mix of books, movies, posters, and stuff like *Harridan Jones for Mayor* buttons that had nothing to do with the Harridan I was interested in.

"Whoa. This will take all day," Dad said.

I shook my head. "Let's refine the search." I added *barbarian* and *number 7*.

"Five matches," Dad said, reading over my shoulder.

"Holy cow!" In the first listing, the book was going for seventy-five dollars. For a moment, I gave up any hopes of ever owning a copy. But then I scanned the rest of the listings. The next one had the book for five dollars. There were two more offered at three fifty, and the last one had numbers seven, eight, and nine in a bundle for twelve bucks.

"Wait," Dad said, pointing to the column between the item description and the current price. "This is how many people made a bid, right?"

I saw what he meant. Nobody had bid seventy-five dollars for the first one. That was just what the guy was asking.

I got Dad to register—he picked the user name Clueless

Stan—and then we put in a bid for one of the copies that was offered at three fifty.

"Let's see what else is for sale," Dad said.

I searched through more of the Harridan listings. "A bunch of people are bidding on number one. Thirty-five dollars for a first edition. Wow."

"Try Dale Gerralds," Dad said. "I've got his early books, from before he was popular. Put that in, and add *first edition*."

"Okay." I did the search and found a dozen listings for first-edition Dale Gerralds books. There were bids as high as forty dollars for one of the titles. "You have this book?"

Dad nodded.

"Wow. Want to sell it?"

Dad shook his head. "I want to hang on to the old books."

"What about some of the other stuff in the basement? You want to try to sell some of it?"

Mom must have been passing by the doorway when I said that. I can't think of any other reason for her to suddenly shout "Hallelujah!"

Dad didn't look like he was going to agree until I said, "If you make money, you can get those parts you want for the

Corvette." Before he could weaken, I pointed toward the basement and added my killer finish. "You saved all that stuff because you knew somebody could use it. Right?"

"Right."

"So, our job is to find that somebody."

I went to the main page and read up on how to sell items. It seemed pretty easy.

"What do you want to sell?" I asked Dad.

"I don't know. Let's look around."

We headed toward the basement. It was somewhere in the hallway that the frenzy began to get into our blood. We started out walking, but as I thought about millions of people bidding money for rare items, I walked faster. Dad kept pace behind me. By the time I reached the steps, I was almost jogging.

Dad and I started pulling things out of boxes and making stacks. "Tennis balls," he said, grabbing the first thing he tripped over.

"Those are old. Who'd want them?"

"Look at the color," he said, holding the can up.

"White?" I asked. "That's weird. Are they so old that they faded?"

"No. They came that way. They don't make 'em that

color anymore. Haven't for years. That's why I kept them. These are unopened, too. Got to be worth something to somebody."

I had my doubts about the tennis balls. But I figured Dad and I were in this together, so I should at least listen to him. We picked five other things to try to sell, too, including some phonograph records and a bunch of typewriter ribbons.

As I was working on the first listing, Mom peeked into my room and said, "Good. You're doing your homework."

I opened my mouth to admit the truth, when a thought smacked me hard enough to make my body twitch. "You'd love it if Dad got rid of some of his junk, right?"

"Love is too weak a word for what I'd feel," she said.

"If I could help him to get rid of a lot of stuff, would you trust me to do my homework without checking it all the time?"

"How much stuff?"

"Lots of it. Tons."

She stood there for a moment, obviously thinking things over. Then she nodded. "If you can do that, you can do anything."

I spent the rest of the day putting the listings up. And the rest of the evening watching my e-mail to see if we got any bids. Dad stuck it out until one A.M., then went to sleep.

"Anything?" he asked the next morning.

"Not yet."

"Not even on the phonograph records?" he asked.

"Especially not on them." I'd noticed that there were thousands of records offered for sale.

Dad shook his head and walked off. I put my head down on my arms and fell asleep. It had been a nice idea, but it looked like online auctions weren't the way to get Dad to clear out his mess, or to get Mom off my back.

When I woke up, I checked the auctions right away. Still no bids. Worse, someone had topped my bid for Harridan number seven. I decided to skip to number eight.

Between reading Harridan novels and watching the auctions, time flew. A week passed, and we didn't get any bids. I couldn't understand it. Someone should have been interested.

I kept studying the auctions, trying to figure out what sold and what didn't. There was some stuff that was obvious. Old Beatles and Elvis stuff sold—but even that had to be rare. Magazines had to be from the 1950s or earlier, unless it was a special issue, like with an assassination or wedding.

Then I noticed something else. There were two people offering the same Beatles album. One had five bids; the other didn't have any. I checked the listings. It was the same album, in the same condition. The only difference was that one person had written a long description of the record. The write-up was so good, it almost made me want to buy the record.

Maybe that was worth a try.

I listed the tennis balls again. My old description just said "Six unopened cans of white tennis balls."

This time, I got creative, did a bit of research, and wrote, "Rare memorabilia from the early days when tennis was a sport played for love instead of money. If you're old enough to remember the glory days of tennis, then you know that tennis balls weren't always so brightly colored. We're fortunate to have recently unearthed six UNOPENED cans of white tennis balls—the same color used by those early legends of the game, Billie Jean King, Rod Laver, and Arthur Ashe. Now, you can own a flawless piece of tennis history."

I posted the listing, then got back to reading Harridan's adventures.

"Did you do your homework?" Mom asked the moment she saw me with the book.

"I thought we had a deal?"

She shook her head. "Not until I see some sort of progress downstairs. Meanwhile, do you have homework?"

"I have a bit of math due for tomorrow," I admitted.

"Get it done before you read."

"I have plenty of time."

She stared at me. I sighed, grabbed my math book, and did the problems. It didn't take long. The instant I was finished, I checked my e-mail. "We got a bid!" I shouted when I saw the subject heading.

Dad came rushing up to my bedroom. "Let's see."

I pointed to the screen. Someone had offered three dollars for the six cans. I pulled up my description on the auction page to show Dad. When I scrolled back to the top, I saw there was a second bid.

By the time the auction ended, we'd sold the cans for $27. I went back to all our unsold items and rewrote the descriptions. They all sold.

Dad and I raided the basement. It became a challenge. He'd pull out some incredibly valueless object and dare me to sell it.

I met every challenge. The floor of the basement started to reemerge. We even found more tennis balls. I spent all of my free time putting up listings. Dad split the money with me, as long as I promised to put half my share away for college. That still left me a nice amount to spend.

Everything went smoothly until a Sunday afternoon at the end of October when Mom came up to my room and said, "I really have to compliment you. You got your dad motivated. And I haven't received any calls from your teachers, so it looks like you've gotten your homework problem under control."

"Yup." I allowed myself a moment of pride as I thought about how well I'd handled everything. I generally knocked off my math during study hall and my history on the bus ride home from school. We'd had hardly any homework in English all through October because of the big project.

Oh, my gosh . . . !

The project . . .

I froze at the keyboard. "English!" I gasped.

"You have English homework?" Mom asked.

I tried to swallow the lump in my throat and then realized it was my tongue. Struggling to keep my voice calm, I said, "Just one thing. No problem." Yeah, it was one thing. A twenty-page report, due tomorrow morning. I glanced at the auction screen, wondering whether anybody was selling

English papers. Or new heads, since mine was about to get ripped off by Mom.

"I'm so proud of you. I thought this day would never come."

Mom smiled, patted me on the head, and left the room. I could feel sweat sprouting from parts of my body that I never knew had sweat glands.

I got up from the computer and wandered into the hall. "This is stupid," I muttered. "I'm not a writer. Why do they give us those assignments?"

"Who's not a writer?" Dad asked, stepping into the hall from his bedroom.

"Me."

He shook his head. "You wouldn't know it—not the way your ads have been pulling in the sales."

My ads! A glimmer of hope threw itself at the towering brick wall of my despair. I might get out of this alive. I minimized my auction screen and opened the folder where I'd kept copies of my item descriptions. I started cutting and pasting. Wow. By the time I'd pulled up everything I'd written, I had over twenty-five pages, even without using my usual trick of pumping up the font.

I added a short introduction. Now all I needed was a title.

That was easy enough. "Descriptive Language as a Means of Sales Motivation." Perfect. I was done with my homework.

I handed my paper in on Monday morning. By Monday afternoon, I was convinced I'd made a horrible mistake. As the week went by, fear and panic danced through all my internal organs. By Thursday, I was sure I'd be in ninth grade forever.

Finally, on Friday, Ms. Cowan gave us back our papers. I didn't get mine. "See me after class," she said.

Oh, boy. That is never a good sign. I spent the whole class imagining the creative words she'd use to describe my pathetic attempt at a project.

As I walked up to her desk after class, I tried to think of the best way to plead for another chance.

"Here," she said, handing me my paper.

I glanced down. It took me a moment to recognize the strange letter and symbol. There was an A+ on the front page. Below it, she'd written the comment, "Wonderful descriptive writing. The examples you came up with to support your hypothesis were excellent. Keep up the good work. You have a flair for promotional prose."

"Thanks." Now I was puzzled. "Why did you want to see me?"

"Those tennis balls you described," she said. "They sound great. I'd love to buy some as a birthday present for my uncle. Do you have any idea where I can get a can?"

"Sure. I'll have to check with my partner, but I think I can take care of that."

I headed out of the classroom, clutching a paper that would keep Mom happy for weeks. I was going to go to the mall after school and buy a calendar organizer so I could keep track of my assignments, but I realized that would be a waste of money. Instead, I went home. Dad had a whole box of organizers in the basement. They were old, but I found one that started out on the same day of the week as this year, which made it perfectly usable. Hey, there are some things you just shouldn't ever throw out.

American Teen

By

Mel Glenn

Here is a cross section of America—stories united not by the interstate, but by the highways of the human heart. Boy, girl, Northerner, Southerner, families split or whole, we see we are pretty much the same, trying to make sense of self, family, neighborhood, and country with humor and courage. More unites us than divides us, and no matter where the individual teen is from, the mountain or the valley, the plains or the seashore, each has to come to terms with him- or herself one story at a time in the human comedy that is our lives.

Allen James (AJ) Martin—*Wichita, Kansas*

My family's driving me crazy.

They're soooo boring!

Here at midmorning,

in my middle school,

in Wichita, Kansas,

in the middle of town,

which is in the middle of the country,*

I am the middle child,

the filling between two slices of white bread

that are my stuck-up older sister,

and my bratty younger one.

My father works for the Midland Bank,

and my mother works part-time as an

account executive for the Midland Hotel.

My parents each drive a midsize sedan,

vote politically the middle of the road.

And we live in the middle of the block.

I am so tired of being in the middle of everything.

I just want to live on the edge.

*If you want to be technical, the exact geographical center
of the country is outside Belle Fourche, South Dakota. I
looked it up, but Kansas is close enough.

Allyson Bass—*Atlanta, Georgia*

In the romantic novels my mother and I read together,
young ladies were invited by fancy invitations
to fancy balls held at fancy palaces and such.
The goal was to find a dashing Mr. Darcy,
one who would be delighted to fill up your dance card
and call formally at your house the next day.
When I told my mother I was going
to my first boy/girl party, a barbecue no less,
she asked me what dress was I going to wear.
"Mom," I said, "we're going to play flag football."
"Jane Austen would never play flag football," my mom said.
"She would collect suitors and then choose the best one."
"C'mon, Mom, things are different today."
"That's for sure. Be careful, honey.
What time will you be home?"

It was the best party ever, loads of food and boys.
I caught three passes, scored a touchdown,

and stopped Bobby Treadwell dead in his tracks.
When I came home, my mom took one look at me,
my skinned knees and grass stains, and said,
"Do remember to write a thank-you note, Allyson.
Ms. Austen would approve of that, I'm sure."

Jaycee Holmes—*Joplin, Missouri*

On our family farm, outside of Joplin,
when there wasn't much to do in the evenings,
we entertained ourselves by singing together after dinner.
My mother said I could carry a tune before I could
    walk.
My father said I sang like a bird before I could talk.
My cousin and assorted relatives believed in me so
    much
there wasn't a local talent contest I didn't win—
pop, blues, rock and roll, I could sing it all.
Visions of recording contracts danced in my head.
You should go on *Idol,* everyone said,
So when the auditions came to St. Louis,
I was dead sure I'd be ticketed for Hollywood.
After waiting all day, it was finally my turn.

"Sketchy," said Randy.

"Sorry, sweetheart," said Paula.

"Simply atrocious," said Simon.

I was totally shocked.

Was everybody in the world lying to me?

I still sing after dinner these days,

But not so loudly anymore.

Darious Knowles—*Philadelphia, Pennsylvania*

Whenever my parents pressure me about

my bad grades,

my bad friends,

my bad social life,

whenever I feel bad about

myself,

my looks,

my height, or lack of it,

I just head for the community pool,

dive in, and swim laps for thirty minutes or more.

I make up rhymes as I pull the water behind me,

pretending I can outlap all my problems.

After my laps, the director approached me.

Hey, what's up, man?
You want me to do what?
Teach a bunch of seventh-graders how to swim?
Yeah, man, I can do that, got my lifeguard certificate.
Thanks for the job, 'ppreciate it.
Yeah, workin' with kids is a fine, fine way
to keep my own head above water.

Kendra Hawkins—*Eau Claire, Wisconsin*

My parents gave me a dog last Christmas,
but to tell you the truth, he don't do too much.
When I wanna go outside and play with him, he looks
at the ball, the stick, the toy, the Frisbee,
then looks at me as if to say,
"You're not serious, are you?
You'd like me, perhaps,
to pull the sled in the Iditarod,
or chase a dumb rabbit round a track?
Forget it, pal, I don't do sports.
Let me instead look at
food, water, treats, bones.
Then maybe we'll do business.

Go get some other dog to play with.

Just put me on the couch, leave me alone,

and let me watch *Oprah*."

Michael Cole—*Sacramento, California*

My father is a teacher.

He teaches social studies in high school.

He works in the den.

My mother is a teacher also.

She teaches fourth-graders.

She works on the kitchen table.

Do I want to be a teacher as well?

No, my dear parents, no.

I want a life without paper and tests.

Every night they both have homework to do,

phone calls, lesson plans, grading.

Even when we go on family vacations

they each carry papers to mark.

"Sorry, Mike, I'll be with you in a minute," my father
    says.

"Sorry, Mike, I need to grade these papers," my mother
    says.

I roll my eyes and turn on my iPod.

My parents are permanently at a distance, it seems,

somewhere far away on assignment.

Jenny Donaldson—*Stephens City, Virginia*

I was just four when my father walked out.

My stepsister was just five when her mother walked out.

When my mother met her father

we were thrown together like ingredients in a witches'
   brew.

We were told in no uncertain terms

we all must get along and be one happy family.

Right.

Cindy hates me, and I hate her.

We blame each other's parents for wrongs committed.

Weekly family meetings to keep the peace

will not make me like her any better.

She borrows my clothes, and I steal her money.

She takes my boyfriends, and I take her girlfriends.

When she enters a room, I leave it, and vice versa.

You could say we are not stepsisters,

we are out of step with each other.

Colby Haas—*Mexico, New York*

My town sounds southern,

as if it were boiling under the summer sun.

Actually, it freezes its ass off every winter,

as if it were a suburb of the North Pole.

It's a place where skaters outnumber sombreros,

a place where the only game in town is hockey,

a poor excuse for local bad boys

to batter each other's brains out on a Saturday
  night.

Every winter, lake-effect snow buries us so deeply

we all might as well hibernate for the duration.

My mother likes the coziness;

my father thinks below-zero windchill promotes
  manliness.

And I think I can't wait to leave this town for good,

find some southern beach and some southern cutie

and make sand angels instead of snow ones.

Home is where the heart is, my mom reminds me,

but how can I feel anything for my hometown

if my heart is frozen solid?

This town just leaves me cold.

Molly Hampton—*Snow Hill, Alabama*

My town sounds northern,

as if it were freezing under the winter sun.

Actually, it sweats its ass off every summer

as if it were a suburb of Death Valley.

It's a place where the fish outnumber the fishermen,

a place where the only game in town is fishing,

a poor excuse for the local bad boys

to get drunk on beer out on the water.

Every summer the searing sun toasts us so deeply

we all might as well loll in the shade for the duration.

My father likes the heat.

My mother thinks the above-ninety temps promote good
    health.

And I think I can't wait to leave this town for good,

find some cool western beach and some California
    hottie

and make waves instead of standing in some boat doin'
    nothing.

Home is where the heart is, my dad reminds me,

But how can I feel anything for my hometown

if my heart is overheated?

This town just burns me up.

Niki Sheridan—*Denver, Colorado*

My parents' slippery marriage
sliding downhill toward divorce
sometimes stops in mid-argument
when my father calls a winter truce:
a family ski trip so that
"we can all get to know each other again,"
an impossible statement said without irony.
His money can't buy happiness,
but it can buy expensive vacations
where hot chocolate and cozy fireplaces
delude us into thinking that my parents' union,
as fragile as snow, will continue along its grooved run.
My parents feel mellow at the inn
and talk about the good old days when I was a baby,
when the future seemed as clear and spotless
as an unskied trail high on the mountain.
While they canoodle on the massive sofa,
saying loving words in front of the roaring fire,
I head for the intermediate hills, embarrassed.
I do not wish to disturb the delicate peace between them.
I smile and think perhaps they just might hold everything
     together,

showing, for a little while longer, where there's life, there's
slope.

Irina Kirov—*Brooklyn, New York*

My father drives livery cab all night.
I see him for brief moment in morning.
When I leave apartment, he enters,
and says in Russian, "Have a good day."
I say same, deliberately in English.
We speak different language in more ways than one.
He wishes he has money enough
to take us all back to home country,
where life is less stressed, he says,
and there is more things to do with family.
When I tell him I wish to stay in U.S.,
and my brother, Andrey, wishes to stay, too,
he says we are children, do not count.
For all I care, he can take cab,
load up my mother and other sister,
drive east, both night and day, back to Ukraine.
It has always been clear to me,
we travel in opposite directions.

Tommy Rosa—*Oklahoma City, Oklahoma*

The thud you heard a couple of years ago
was me hitting rock bottom.
I failed my subjects.
I failed my teachers.
I failed myself, all by myself.
Everyone on the known planet
put distance between themselves and me,
everyone except my parents, that is.
I did drugs—they took me to rehab.
I got arrested for shoplifting—they bailed
  me out.
No matter how far I fell,
they caught me in their safety net,
saying I still had time to do good.
Even though I tried to push them outta my life,
they always hung around the edges
waiting for me to return to my better self.
They continue to love and prop me up
as I continue the long climb back up.
I used to think they were so stupid.
How'd they get so smart?

Carrie Nyland—*Tacoma, Washington*

My mother always wants to go shopping with me

to these large outlet stores way out of the city

that look like airplane hangars.

For her, shopping is a blood sport,

the thrill of the hunt for a bargain.

She insists it's a good bonding experience

    for us—

so how come I don't want to shop with her

    anymore?

The truth is, I'd rather be with my friends.

"The stores just rip you off," I say,

not telling her the real reason.

"You're so jaded," she says, disappointed.

"Where is my little girl who couldn't wait

to go shopping with me?"

How do I tell her

I am no longer her little girl

without hurting her feelings?

How do I tell her

my friends are more fun than she is?

I think my mother has to shop around for someone

    else.

Marlene Esterhaus—*Columbus, Ohio*

My mother was not amused when

I was twelve, and on my own

I got my ears pierced.

"Who knows if they used a clean needle?" she wailed.

My mother was less than thrilled when

I was fifteen, and on my own

I got my eyebrow pierced.

"Who told you a pincushion

constitutes a fashion statement?" she cried.

When I had my belly button pierced,

she tried sarcasm to no avail.

"My, honey, isn't that a navel experience?"

Last week, on my seventeenth birthday,

I got my other eyebrow pierced.

"What are you, a human dartboard?" she shouted.

"It's my body—I can do what I want," I shot back.

What I'd really like to get is a lip ring

and my tongue pierced with a sixty-five-dollar

    miniature barbell.

How do I tell my mother that?

I'm afraid the news would leave her totally

tongue-tied.

Judi Herbst—*Plano, Texas*

When I wanted to try out for the cheerleading squad,
my mother said, "You've got a good heart."
But I'd gladly trade that body part
for the two that mean so much more to teenage boys,
especially those boys who happen to play football.
My friend says, "You've got a good personality,"
but I'd gladly trade that character trait
for the body parts I didn't specifically mention above.
When boys look at you, they don't look at you.
They look lower, and if you catch them staring,
they say something stupid like
"Did you lose weight?"
My mother says I will develop in time.
It's not all that important, she adds.
Yeah, right, Mom.
When was the last time you tried out for
    cheerleading?
When was the last time you were fourteen?
When was the last time you had to worry about that?
Sorry to go off on you like that.
But, hey, thanks for letting me get this
off my chest.

Noah Rossen—*Baltimore, Maryland*

Across a table, kitchen or restaurant,

across a field, soccer or baseball,

I can still see my father

in his Oriole cap and college sweatshirt.

Across a room, dining or kitchen,

across a street, East Pratt or Light,

I can still sense my father holding my hand

as we walk along the Inner Harbor.

My mother feeds me slices of memories:

how he played catch with me,

how he took me to Camden Yards.

I wish I remembered more about him.

Slivers of old photos, crumbs of old home
     videos

can't bring him back into a sharper focus.

My best friend, Alan, says he can't speak to his
     father.

What a joke. Your father's alive.

My father died when I was seven.

Alan's memories get refreshed daily,

while mine have stopped, framed and frozen
     forever.

Carter Bishop—*Converse, Louisiana*

Basketball's not only the king in Converse—
it's the whole damn royal court.
If you want to know, I don't particularly care for
    b-ball,
but a statement like that is treason round here.
My father, the owner of the feed store in town,
played for our high school team before
he went to Nam and got shot up.
He doesn't talk much about his injuries,
but rather talks about the fights he had
with our division rivals over in Ebarb.
"I once scored forty-three points against 'em," he said.
"I think it was a parish record for about five years."
Once in a while my father fakes left, goes right
down the aisles where the fertilizer bags sit,
but it's like he's movin' in super–slow mo.
"Goin' to the game Friday?" he asks,
ever hopeful that I will catch the basketball bug.
"Don't think so," I say. My father turns from me
and rearranges some cans on the shelf,
perhaps aware that the final horn has sounded
on the playing field of his teenage dreams.

Rich Langham—*Preston, Idaho*

I get up before sunrise to milk the cows,
who look like rumpled children before waking up.
Our dairy farm outside of Preston
tends to milk us dry in the lean years.
But my father, cursing luck and weather,
refuses to give up and tells me one day
the farm'll be mine, no matter what I want.
I tell him I want to be in the rodeo,
go on the circuit, riding and wrestling.
"That's a lot of bull," he says, thinkin' he's funny.
"What am I workin' for?" he shouts.
"So you can be some kind of cowboy
and have no responsibilities at all?
Life ain't like that, son—you're actin' crazy."
I tell him I don't wanna look at
the back ends of cows my whole life.
"Go, then," he says. "Go right now. I don't need
   you."
"Dad, I don't mean right now. Besides—"
"We'll talk about this later, maybe never," he says,
   turning.
"The cows need milking now."

"But, Dad—"
"We'll talk about this later, I said."

Julien Nieves—*Omaha, Nebraska*

Javi saw Iraq as a giant football field.
There were offensive and defensive lines,
constantly shifting in day and night maneuvers,
soldiers advancing on long drives,
gaining ground, yard by precious yard,
with mortars thrown in the flat,
bombs hurled toward the red zone and
holes opened up in enemy lines.
"All true," he told us when he came home on leave.
"You don't think too much, just listen to the signals
    given.
You just try to push back the other side."
We urged him not to re-up for another season,
but he brushed us off like a speck on his uniform,
told us he wanted to be out there for the victory
    celebration.
We learned later, while still at our books,
he fell to the ground, blindsided by an attack he
    never saw.

He never knew whether his squad won or lost,
as if that mattered in the final score.
He was too young to know the rules of the game.
I will always treasure and remember my brother
for his valor on the field of battle.

Donna Capisella—*Boston, Massachusetts*
I don't even hear the T anymore
as I lie on my bed and think
I would rather have my parents
fighting in the same house than being
icily civil to each other in separate apartments.
I miss their cursing out each other.
I miss their throwing things, dishes mostly.
I miss the slammed doors, the overturned furniture,
as they fought over my future, athletic or academic.
My father thinks I can get a basketball scholarship
    at BU.
My mother thinks I can go to MIT,
but after one fight too many about how
my father wanted to turn me into a jock,
and my mother wanted to turn me into a nerd,
the tip of the mountain of arguments between them,

they got a divorce, sold the house,

and moved to different sides of the track,

where I became the commuter between stations

   A and B.

I have two rooms now, two of everything.

I'd much rather have one of everything, even though

I'd have to endure the train wreck of their lives.

Jay Harpring—*Scottsdale, Arizona*

Yeah, I know it's corny to say,

but my father IS my pal.

He's usually an easygoing guy,

someone I enjoy being around.

We play golf together pretty regularly.

When my putts were falling, one graying afternoon,

and his were just lipping the cup,

he didn't get too excited, but said with a tight smile,

"Tiger better watch his step."

"Jeez, Dad, I'm lucky, that's all," I said,

trying to make him feel better.

"No, you're good.

You better go home now, looks like rain."

"Aren't you coming?" I said.

"In a while," he said.
I started to walk off the green, turned
and looked over my shoulder.
He was hitting putt after putt,
not paying attention to the rain hitting his
    Windbreaker,
the smile fading from his lips.

Karen Glasgow—*Minot, North Dakota*
My mother has always stood
in the theater wings of my life,
pushing me onstage before
I was ready to perform on my own.
She has always urged me to try out for different roles.
"Of course you should try out for the musical, honey.
I played the lead in every production,
from sophomore year on, you know."
Of course I know, given her constant monologues,
presented center stage for my instruction.
"I got fabulous reviews in the papers, you know."
How could I not? She has cued my lines
to the point where I don't even know
if I control my own voice.

She stage-manages me so skillfully
that I continue to act as the understudy to her life.
She upstages me in front of my friends,
telling jokes and stories that make her the star.
She doesn't act her age—she acts mine,
constantly reprising her leading roles.
I'm afraid she will always seek the spotlight,
pushing me permanently into the background.

Danny Asadorian—*Taos, New Mexico*
(*formerly of Chicago*)
My mother shed my father like an old winter coat,
left the winds of Chicago and headed
for the sands of New Mexico.
My mother shed her safe office job for
the risky sun-dappled life of an artiste and
took me in tow like some remembered piece of
    luggage.
I feel a stranger in this strange land of browns and coral.
I miss the roar of the El in the Loop,
the roar of the crowds at Wrigley,
and the cold slap of winter on my face.
"How can you not like this open sky?" she asks.

"I feel like an alien," I say.

"Go make friends—just walk outside."

"No one speaks English," I cry.

Banished, I walk over to the local Mexican
restaurant,

where Maria, her name emblazoned on her blouse,

asks me in Spanish what I would like.

¿Qué quiere usted?

Is she talking about food or my life? I think,

feeling lost in two languages.

Jocelyn Lanier—*Presque Isle, Maine* (*originally*)

I had come to the city all the way from Presque Isle,

a town so far north it might as well be in Canada.

With a Greyhound passport, I came to Port Authority

in the Big Apple, despite my mother, who said,

"What can you find in New York?"

I was too polite to answer "A life?"

"Don't think you can just come back so easy," she said.

I looked for a small place to stay on streets

too numerous to have their own names, just a letter.

Staying at the Y, I answered an ad for a waitress job,

at the Aztec diner, on Sixth, just temporary, I thought.

Now I pour a second cup of coffee for the regulars
and look outside the big glass window
at the professional people who rush by.
My mother hardly calls anymore,
as if the distance between us were only miles.
In my stubbornness, I hardly call her, too,
afraid to admit the rashness of my decision to leave.
I pick up still another order of two eggs over well,
while feeling the pain of my tired feet,
and the pain of my mother not talking to me.

Lucas Breen—*Charleston, South Carolina*
My grandfather, before he died,
liked to walk with me along East Bay Street.
We would watch the ships sail in and out of the
    harbor,
and he would tell me stories of his travels round the
    world.
My grandfather, late of the merchant marines,
sailed into peaceful Freetown on the west coast of Africa,
before the rebels hacked their way through the bush,
and before they hacked the hands and arms of little
    children.

He'd shop in the markets for country cloth,
and would find his way to the old City Hotel,
where he'd sit on the verandah and drink Star beer.
When I was young, he would teach me sea and sky,
showing me how to plot a course from A to B.
I've always tried to follow the straight course he laid out
    for me.
I've always tried to follow his moral northern star,
especially on the broken ship of my parents' marriage.
One day, I will go to Freetown and drink Star beer
on the verandah of the old City Hotel,
that is, if the coast is clear.

Antoine Johnson—*Detroit, Michigan*
I never argue with my father.
I think it strange that
I can never hear his voice in my ear.
He walks the house in slippered quiet.
He eats without conversation at the dinner table,
hardly ever asking about my day at school.
He buries himself nightly in the big TV chair
and does the daily crossword puzzle in ink.
Sometimes, I think he is held willing prisoner

by the regiment of words marching across his lap.

"Don't bother your father," my mother says.

"He's had a hard day at the plant.

They're letting people go."

What words, I wonder,

across and down, does he have for me?

Some advice, maybe,

that will help me understand

the mysterious puzzle of myself.

Those words do not leap off his page.

Laura Baines—*Ogden, Utah*

I always argue with my mother.

I think it strange that

I always hear her voice in my ear.

Soldier Boy, my parents aren't

exactly thrilled with our new relationship.

They worry you'll get shot and stuff,

and don't want me to wind up alone.

My parents can't stop us from seeing each other.

My parents can't stop what is meant to be.

When you're overseas, fighting for freedom,

I'll spend English class writing you letters,

math class figuring ways I can see you,

social studies class pinpointing you on a map.

I'll be so proud of you with medals on your chest.

No distance can keep us apart.

I don't care what my parents say;

we were meant for each other.

Soldier Boy, you are my man.

God bless the U.S. of A.

Chantelle Pierce—*Memphis, Tennessee*

My mother thinks I'm a virgin.

I was—two years ago.

The less she knows about my social life,

the more she can live in the past.

How can I tell her about Thomas,

who took my hand and then worked his way

'cross other parts of my anatomy,

exploring the landscape like some misguided
     traveler?

His intention was always to sightsee, never
     bothering

to check the feelings of the local inhabitant.

He promised to call from the road

when he somehow "found himself."

But apparently he ran out of gas and interest,

so, reluctantly, I dropped him because

our relationship was stuck in neutral.

I hope to get better mileage out of someone new,

someone less scared of the journey together,

someday when I am fit for travel.

In the meantime, I'll just go on vacation with my mom.

I think I'll be a lot better off,

as long as we don't discuss my social life.

Briana Sue Sachs—*Portland, Oregon*

Looking in the attic of the old house,

a beautiful pink house on SE Salmon Street,

the one that you and great-grandpa lived in for forty
    years,

I found a picture of you, standing on skis

atop a mountain, I think it's in Austria.

You must have been my age then, fifteen or so.

You were smiling and happy with your friend,

ready to rush down the mountain of your life,

confident in negotiating the twists and turns,

of poverty, war, and relocation,

coming to America to start a new life in the Rose City.

I sit at your parlor window now,

the one overlooking your favorite rosebushes,

and think of your wild ride down the mountain,

wishing I could hear more of your European stories,

and hoping, too, I can become half the woman you were.

Paul Dennison—*Buxton, North Carolina*

My family's driving me crazy.

They are soooo strange!

Here at the edge of the East Coast,

at Cape Hatteras Secondary School

in Buxton, North Carolina,

which is at the edge of the water,

at the eastern end of the Outer Banks,*

I am the firstborn, who has all the responsibility

to watch my three sisters, all below ten years of age,

who usually get on my nerves

and never listen to what I say.

My father used to work for Eastern Airlines.

My mother works part-time as a

group sales rep for the Eastern Hotel.

My parents drive a Subaru, made in the Far East,

vote politically for the eastern establishment.

And we live in a house facing east toward the water.

I am so tired being at the edge of the country.

Maybe when I grow up, I'll just travel west toward the
    sunset.

*If you want to be technical, the easternmost point of the
country is Lubec, Maine. I looked it up, but North Carolina is close enough.

The Most Mauve There Is

By

Nancy Springer

The true horror of my situation didn't hit me until the family females took us family males to be measured for our "formalwear." Up till then, I thought my sister's wedding, and her sugar-brained idea of what I was supposed to do in it, would just go away, you know? She was always breaking up with guys, so what made this Mark whatsisface any different? I hadn't been paying much attention.

But what I saw in the Tuxedos And More store woke me up so fast I freaked.

"I'm not! I won't! You can't do this to me!" I yelled when they brought out my "ensemble"—shiny black buckle shoes like Christopher Robin wore going to visit Winnie-the-Pooh, white stockings, short pants with black ribbon bows at the knees, a little bitty black jacket with *tails*, and a white shirt with *ruffles*. I'm thirteen years old, for gosh sake. "Ewww! I'd rather be the flower girl!"

"Hush up, Avery Alexander." Mom's use of my first and middle name signaled an orange level of alert for potential parental terrorism. Quick, I checked Dad, but the look on his face didn't belong there. My father's all about taking charge, so why did he seem, like, helpless?

"*I'm* the flower girl!" screeched my brat kid sister, who always takes everything seriously. "*I* get to scatter the rose petals! Valerie said!"

"Shhh, Julie," Mom told her a lot more gently than she had shushed me. "Of course you're the flower girl. Avery's just being—"

I cut her off. "I'm just being sane! Get some little kid who won't care. I'm too big to be a ring bearer!"

"You're small for your age," said Mom, like my being the midget of middle school was real helpful. I'd been told that as a kid Dad had been undersized, too, till he had a growth spurt and shot up a foot in one year.

"I don't mean *that* kind of too big!"

"I know exactly what you mean, Avery Alexander, and my response is, suck it up."

"Easy for you to say! *You* don't have to face my friends." When my Avery-hating girl cousins got me in the sights of their cell phone cameras, and everybody in school saw me wearing—

"You've got to be kidding!" I yelped as the Tuxedos And More lady, a large woman with hair like coils of steel wire, bent over and put a big satin thing around my waist. "What's that?"

"Your cummerbund. To go with your Little Lord Fauntle-roy tie."

"But it's *pink*!"

"Not pink," Mom snapped. "Mauve."

Julie whined, "But you told me my dress is going to be pink! I like pink!"

"Mauve is a very special kind of pink."

I'll say. Like the color you might get if a pink cat coughed up a hairball.

Here came the metal-haired lady with the tie, another huge satin monstrosity made of pink ribbon in a bow. I jumped back. "I'm not doing it!" My voice came out deep at first but slipped up into a squeak; I hate that. "Not if I have to wear this stuff! It's not natural!"

"Avery," said Dad with a sigh, "if I have to wear a monkey suit with a pink vest and a pink tie—"

"What sort of family are you!" my big sister, Valerie, burst out. Up till then she'd just been standing around holding Mark's hand and looking like he was the pancake and she was the maple syrup. But all at once there she was in our faces, leaking tears, aiming big, wet eyes at Dad and me. Mostly at me. "All my life I've dreamed of having a real Victorian wedding," she bleated like a weepy sheep, "with satin and lace and roses and *mauve*, which is the most Victorian color there is and my favorite color in the whole world, with my little sister as flower girl and my little brother as ring bearer—is that too much to ask?"

"Of course not," Mom said right on cue. "It'll be your day, Valerie, and you'll have it just the way you want." She turned on me. "Avery Alexander Holsopple, not another word out of you." Three names; threat level red. "Stand still and let the lady take your measurements."

So there I stood, as helpless as if they had handcuffed me, not so much because of my mom's warning as because of the hurt-lambie look in my sister's eyes. That look gets me every time, and I hate it. I let that wire-for-hair woman put her tape measure all over me, and I didn't say another word, but I thought of plenty. Harsh ones. Especially when I saw that the groom, Mark, didn't have to wear pink, or mauve, whatever; he had a *white* tie and vest with his tux. I glared at him the whole evening after that. I hated him. Why'd he have to marry my sister?

When I said my wedding outfit wasn't natural, what I meant was, all my life I've been running around the farm—Holsopple Orchard, Fine Apples, Peaches, Plums, Apricots—and fishing in the creek and swimming in the pond and taking care of cows, goats, Julie's pony, whatever, and helping with the work; that's what I mean by natural.

And dogs. I've always been good with dogs. We adopt stray dogs, and I train them to come when they're called, sit and stay, keep off the road, and leave the chickens alone even when nobody's looking.

We had three mutts, and a few days after Tuxedos And

More, I was taking them for a long walk to get away from all the mayhem, melodrama, and mauve in the house: tables piled with ribbons and fake flowers and lace so a person had to eat standing up over the sink, no place to sit because in every chair was one of my aunts making velvet roses or fancy pink fans, Valerie running around with fake ivy, decorating everything except the toilet seat, and yelling at me not to track in any dirt, keep the house clean, clean, *clean* for the wedding, which was going to be inside if it rained but she hoped outside under the apple trees.

"That makes a lot of sense," I remarked. "We're supposed to dress up all Victorian to go tramping through a field?"

"Hush up, Avery," ordered my mom, who was trying to bake, from original Victorian recipes, the worst cookies I ever was told not to eat, while Julie paraded around with a frilly basket practicing how to be a flower girl, and my cousins, the ones with the deadly cell phones, showed off their high heels and long dresses—how come *they* got to be bridesmaids but I wasn't a groomsman?

I was the ring bearer. I was supposed to carry the rings on a pillow. Satin. Mauve. With lace hanging down from the edges.

The whole thing had me so bummed that, walking through the shadowy old part of the orchard, I didn't look up until all three dogs started barking.

I told the mutts to hush, but when I saw who was jogging toward me between the rows of gnarly trees, I wished they'd bite him. It was Mark.

"Hi, Avery," he puffed as he caught up with me. Had he, like, followed me?

"What do you want? Why aren't you down at the house sucking face with my sister?" Finally, I had a chance to be rude to let him know how extensively I didn't like him—I mean, what was to like? There was nothing special about Mark that I could see, no reason for Valerie to put me through mauve-colored hell so she could marry him. He wasn't a football player or anything like that, just an average sort of geek.

But he didn't seem to mind my dissing him at all. "I want to talk with you," he answered, keeping up with me easily no matter how fast I tried to walk away. "I want to ask you for some advice. Val tells me you're really, really good with dogs?"

Huh.

"Well, yeah, I guess," I muttered.

"Well, that's awesome. I don't know a thing about dogs, but I'd like for Val and me to have one. I thought I might get her one for a wedding present."

"Yeah?" I still wanted to be rude, but I have to admit I was interested.

"Yeah. But my question is, what kind? See, it would have to be a Victorian sort of dog."

Under the circumstances, the words *Victorian* and *dog* together in one sentence made me groan out loud and say something I can't repeat.

"Yeah, I know," Mark agreed placidly, "but Val has reasons for wanting a Victorian wedding. Did she ever tell you?"

No, she hadn't. Actually, I'd never thought to ask.

"Val says her main skill as a person is boiling apple butter," Mark went on. "All her life she's been doing that, or gathering eggs or butchering beef or shoveling manure. Which is fine—but for just this one day she'd like to get away from all that, the manure end of things, especially, and be different. Just for her wedding she wants to be a lady."

We walked out from under the hunchbacked old apple trees and started through a newer part of the orchard with more sunlight. I still felt like my sister was stupid but maybe not Mark so much. I wished I could think of something to say, but my mind was in kind of a mess.

"So, anyway," Mark went on after a while, "what kind of dog would a Victorian lady like?"

And, get this, the mess in my mind cleared up. Right away I knew the answer. "A lap dog. Maybe a papillon or a Pekingese or a bichon frise. Something cute and little and fluffy, and probably it should be white, unless you want to dye it mauve."

He laughed so hard I had to smile as he asked, "Could we do that? Really?"

"It probably wouldn't be good for the dog."

"Then we won't," he said. "But listen, here's what I was thinking. . . ."

We walked and talked for quite a while. By the time we headed back toward the house, I had a whole new outlook on the wedding and a very different, much better opinion of Mark.

"Are you sure?" I asked him last thing before we went back inside to all the mauve mayhem.

"Yeah, I'm sure," he said. "It's my wedding, too, isn't it? Don't worry, Avery, I take full responsibility."

He held up his hand, and I gave him a high five.

The first really cool part wasn't even planned. It just happened, the day of the wedding—which, luckily for everybody, turned out sunny, the way Valerie wanted it. I put on my ring-bearer outfit and went downstairs for inspection. There stood Val in her white princess bride dress, satin skirt big enough for a parachute, and lace up to her ears, with her hair piled on top of her head full of flowers. She looked like a real lady—but she sure didn't sound like a lady when she saw me and screamed, "Oh, my God!" Her freshly manicured hands flew to her professionally made-up face. "Avery!" she wailed.

"What?" I hadn't even done anything yet, just thrown on my "ensemble," ruffles and ribbons and all, not caring because it didn't matter anymore—but Val didn't know that, and I had to keep acting like I hated her wedding.

So I scowled while my sister looked like she was going to cry. "Avery Holsopple, you must have grown three inches since they measured you!"

Whoa. My growth spurt at last? I stood up taller, and it was hard not to grin.

"Mom!" Valerie yelled toward the kitchen. "Ma! C'mere, please! I don't know what to do. Avery looks like a scarecrow!"

Mom came out with her biggest apron covering her mother-of-the-bride gown, looked me up and down, then said, "Oh, dear."

Julie came out too, all angelic in her fluffy mauve flower-girl dress, that is if angels say, "Ew."

"His bony wrists are sticking out!" Val wailed. "The jacket's short! The knickerbockers don't cover his knees!"

"I *told* you to get some little kid!" I was starting to feel bad for her, and I hate that.

"Avery Alexander, hush," Mom said, turning to Valerie. "Honey, don't worry about it. Nobody will notice."

"The heck they won't!" It was time for me to throw my fit.

Mom ignored me, telling the teary-eyed bride, "They'll all be looking at *you.*"

"Fine!" I yelled. "Then I don't have to be there!"

"Yes, you do!" Mom snapped at me.

"Avery, I'm sorry!" cried Valerie at the same time, which was the last thing in the world I expected her to say, and it really upset me. Why'd she have to turn human just when I needed her to be a pain? She was ruining everything, making me want to hug her and tell her it was okay when I was supposed to be throwing a tantrum. I couldn't even remember what to say, so I just yelled, "You *ought* to be sorry!" then ran upstairs to my room and slammed the door.

And locked it.

Whew.

Thank God that part was done. It was time to put the rest of the plan in motion.

"Okay, Secret," I whispered, opening my closet, "you can come out now."

She pricked up her ears like she understood every word, and I swear to God she smiled at me. Victorian Secret—that's what Mark and I named her—was not only the cutest little curly-haired white lap dog that ever lived, but she was *smart*. I should know. I'd been spending hours with Mark, helping him train her, and she was as quick as any dog I ever met.

Mark didn't do too bad either; he seemed almost as smart as Secret.

All shampooed and sweet-smelling, she zinged spring-loaded out of the carrier I'd used to sneak her into the house, circled my room a couple of times to get the bounces out, then hopped onto my bed, ready for whatever.

Somebody knocked at my bedroom door. Secret didn't bark. She never barked, which was a good thing, because Valerie didn't want any barking during her wedding. Our dogs were staying at another farm for the day.

I'm the one who barked. At the door. "What!" Making sure I sounded really bratty and pissed off.

"Avery." As I expected, it was my dad. Mom had sent him up to talk to me. "Open up."

"No." Mouthier than I ever could have done it if it was for real. "What do you want?"

"Avery Alexander Holsopple." But Dad didn't sound threat level red like he should have; he just sounded tired. "You come out of there. The preacher's here. It's almost time to start."

I knew that, because through my bedroom window I could see the back field with rented chairs facing a kind of stage loaded with flowers. I could see people in their best clothes being shown to their chairs by ushers in black tuxedos with mauve vests and ties. I could see the string quartet playing.

"I'll be down when I'm darn good and ready!" I yelled at my father.

"You'd better be down when *Valerie* is ready. You have the rings in there, don't you?"

"Yes!"

"You better come on down *now.*"

"I'll *be* there! When I have to! And not a minute sooner!"

"Why is it," Dad said in that weary tone he'd been using a lot lately, "that a wedding invariably brings out the utmost lunacy in every member of any given family?"

"Go away," I told him.

Without much heart, more like he was programmed to do it, Dad lectured my door about attitude, maturity, consideration for other people, et cetera, but finally he had to leave, because Mom and Val were calling him.

Meanwhile, I opened my back window a crack so I'd be able to hear what was going on. Also, being quiet so nobody would realize I was on the move, I took off my big floppy pink bow tie and put it onto Secret's neck instead. It looked a heck of a lot cuter on her than it did on me. Made me smile, and I grinned even wider as I took off my pink cummerbund and put it on her too. It looked like a fancy silk skirt. Now she was all ready except for the rings.

I tiptoed to my closet to get the basket—Mark and I had sneaked Julie's flower-girl basket to a craft store and found a little Secret-sized basket just like it, plus the right kinds of frilly stuff we needed to fix it up. We'd spent an evening making fun of each other while we decorated it with lace. And ribbon. Mauve.

So there was Secret's basket, with the rings in it on a little satin pillow Mark had rigged. I checked to make sure they were there—yeah. Two gold rings, one for the bride and one for the groom.

Meanwhile, from underneath my bedroom window I could hear the voices of the wedding party getting organized inside the screen porch. "We might have to do it without Avery," Mom was saying.

"We can't!" Valerie wailed. "He has the rings!"

"I could go break his door down and drag him out here by the ears." Dad sounded like he almost meant it.

"No, don't, Mr. Holsopple. Please." That was Mark, all earnest. "Avery is going to be my brother-in-law. I don't want to get off to a bad start with him—"

My jaw dropped. So did the ring basket, almost, as I realized something, standing there with my mouth airing.

"—and when he says he'll be here on time, I believe him," Mark went on. "I think we ought to trust him. Let's go ahead. Okay? Valerie?"

She must have agreed, because I heard the music change.

I patted Secret and watched from my window as Mark walked out into the field.

"That sneaky geek," I whispered in admiration, because now I understood that Mark had been doing *me* a favor, not Val or himself, by getting a certain wedding present for his bride. "He may be even smarter than you, huh, Secret?" I ruffled the curls on the little dog's head.

The groomsmen followed Mark like ducks in tuxes, all of them taking their places in a line by the preacher, who had been standing there waiting. I watched while the ushers escorted my mother and Mark's mom and dad to front-row seats. Then the music changed again, for the bridesmaids to sail down the aisle like more ducks, mauve, in a row. Next, the flower girl was supposed to go, strewing rose petals for the bride—the main event—who would then walk down the aisle on her father's arm.

The ring bearer was supposed to be with the flower girl.

I waited until the bridesmaids got started, then patted Secret, picked her up in one hand and her basket in the other, and ran downstairs and out to the screen porch. Julie, Val, and Dad all heard me coming and turned to tell me what they thought of me, but when they saw where my cummerbund and bow tie had got to, their mouths opened and just stayed that way. With a big grin, I bowed like a magician.

"Go ahead, Julie," I told my sister as I crouched to put Secret on the floor, giving her the little ring basket to carry in her mouth.

Julie did—she followed the bridesmaids down the aisle the way she was supposed to, but she was so flummoxed that she forgot to strew her rose petals until she got to the end, when she turned her basket over and dumped the petals all in a pile in front of the stage.

Behind me, Valerie was making funny little noises. I couldn't tell whether she was laughing or crying. And I couldn't look, because I had a dog to handle.

I told Secret, "Go to Mark," and opened the screen porch door. She bounced out with her basket in her mouth, and Mark snapped his fingers so she spotted him, and just the way we'd trained her, she trotted right up the aisle, incidentally scattering rose petals with her paws before she sat down beside Mark's shiny patent-leather heel, still holding her basket in her mouth.

While everybody out there in the chairs was oohing at pretty pink Julie and aahing at too-cute-to-shoot Victorian Secret, my sister finally got her voice back and said, "Avery Alexander Holsopple." She sounded like she didn't know whether to smack me or hug me. "What is that dog doing in my wedding?"

"Ask Mark," I told her as I turned around, but then I just stood there staring at her and Dad. Valerie looked so different, tears on her face but also a glow, it's hard to describe. Kind of like she was all sunrise inside. And Dad—well, for the first time in weeks, Dad didn't look tired. Or helpless. He was smiling. He wouldn't look at me, but he was grinning like his team had just scored a touchdown.

The string quartet started to play that "Here Comes the Bride" music.

"I'll wait here till you get up front," I told Val. "Go ahead. Get married."

"I will. Thank you ever so much for your permission." She gave me the funniest smile. Then she looked at Dad, got all serious again, and off they went. Everybody stood up and craned their necks to watch as he walked her down the aisle and handed her over to Mark.

"Dearly beloved," the preacher started, "we are gathered here today to join this man and this woman in holy matrimony. . . ."

I sneaked to a seat in the back, feeling kind of weird— not because of my stupid outfit; I didn't care anymore what I looked like. It was that "holy matrimony" thing making me kind of dizzy, a little bit off balance, like my sister was going away into a different dimension of life. When she went up on the stage with Mark and turned so I could see her face, she looked so, like, beautiful in a way I never saw before, so kind of uplifted, that she seemed like a stranger to me, like she was leaving the farm behind and nothing was ever going to be the same again—

Just then, Secret stood up, set the ring basket down beside Mark, trotted down the steps of the stage and ran off toward a vacant part of the field. Where the grass was taller.

And the whole wedding stopped while everybody watched, not sure what to do, as the little white dog—

Picked a spot to squat.

Oh, no. Oh, man, Val was never going to forgive me. I wished I could just disappear into the earth like dog pee. I tried to tell myself it wasn't my fault my crazy sister got married in a dog's bathroom, and Secret was a good girl, excusing herself. After she finished her business, she ran right back to Mark, like, okay, let's get on with it. Smart little dog. I heard people chuckling while I cringed, I covered my eyes, afraid to look at my sister's face—

But, talk about utmost lunacy, Valerie started laughing! Really laughing, warm and happy. When I looked, Val was picking up her new, furry ring bearer and hugging her. She didn't put Secret down again until it was time to do the vows and the rings. Then, when the wedding was over, Val came up the aisle and back to the house with a husband in one hand and her bouquet plus a little white dog in the other.

"Avery," she said the minute she saw me, "would you for gosh sake get out of that ridiculous outfit? Go put on your church clothes or something."

So finally, no more mauve melodrama; things were back to normal. Except better, because Mark gave me a high five.

Tunnel Vision

By

John H. Ritter

I had the perfect family. Just me, my parents, and a baseball lover's life.

Then I died.

Blam! Just like that. At the baseball park, a half hour before our game against the Mudsuckers, I keeled over. Well, to be honest, I had a little help from our team's best hitter, Charlie Musselwhite.

I was playing catch with Speedy Santos, the only kid on

the team punier than me, and dreaming about being a baseball hero. Usual stuff. Charlie stood behind me, in foul ground, facing the stands. He was acting cool, taking massive swings with his big black thirty-four-inch bat, while radio-announcing each cut.

"There it goes, folks! Musselwhite just muscled another one over the wall!"

It was all just a show for Mandy Bogdonovich, who sat in the bleachers, pretty much ignoring him, while giggling and "oh-my-godding" back and forth with Lola Vertalucci. I didn't know why he'd even bother. Mandy's about as bright as a key chain light, but Charlie's kind of a dim bulb himself, so it maybe makes sense.

Lola, on the other hand, is the sunshine of my *puni*verse. She is my corolla. She drives me out of *controlla*. And one day I'm going to get around to telling her how I feel. I mean, if I ever get a chance.

Anyway, there I was playing catch with Speedy and dreaming what it'd be like if I were Charlie, if I were strong enough to wield his mighty weapon. To feel, just once, what it'd be like to connect with that humongous bat. To send a bright white ball sailing off into the wild blue yonder and see Lola jumping up and down and going all bonkers.

That's when Speedy launched a throw way over my head. A bloopin' rocketship.

But no sweat. I focused on it like a dog chasing a Frisbee at the beach, using pure tunnel vision, like my dad's always telling me to do "when you want to get things done." I turned and bolted off. You should've seen me. Like Derek Jeter in action.

As Dad would say, "Good hustle." But as Mom would say, "Bad choice, Peter."

With my vision narrowed on the ball, I ran headfirst smack into the follow-through of Charlie's gigantic swing. *Fore*head first, to be exact. Not sure what happened next, but as I went flying sideways, a part of me—like, the movie-camera part of my brain—just flew up into the sky.

It was the most bizarre thing. I looked down and could see my own body, sprawled out in foul territory. I saw everybody gather around. Saw Charlie crouch down and say, "Hey, Petey. Sorry, dude. You all right?"

Yeah, sure, Sherlock. Find a clue. For example, *the blood*.

Funny thing was, I actually did seem to be doing all right, floating up there where I was—wherever I was.

Everybody started talking at once. "Call 9-1-1!" "Is he breathing?" "Check his pulse."

"Whoa," said Speedy, who despite his name was not actually all that swift. "Look at his face. Dude, I don't know."

"Gimme room," Coach yelled. "I know CPR."

Don't bother, I wanted to say, after swooping down to take a better look. Who wants to be known as Flathead for the rest of your life?

I floated back up, pop-fly high, where things turned even weirder. A huge globe of rainbow-colored "electricity," about the size of a basketball, came zooming up, buzzing my head. Then another. Then a third. For a moment, these glowing globes wobbled and crackled in front of me before stretching into shimmering, almost liquid, shafts of light. Which started to take shape.

Human shapes.

The lights morphed into three guys, all about my age, floating in the air wearing silky blue and white baseball uniforms. And even though they had transitioned into solid-looking, 3-D beings, they weren't really all that solid. They quivered and glimmered from their ball caps down to their cleats, as though I was looking at their reflections in a pond.

"Pete! Hey, Peter!" they called all at once. "Good to see

you, dude." They swarmed around me like old friends, patting my back, ruffling my hair.

"Who are you guys?" I asked.

The tallest one, with teeth like a horse, answered. "I'm Abe. That's Marty. And the little guy's JJ. You know. Your cousins from Kentucky."

"Cousins from where?" I said, though I didn't actually speak. Turns out, all I had to do was "impulse" the thought to them, and they heard me perfectly.

The middle-sized one, Marty, whose blond hair draped down both sides of his face, prodded my memory. "Christmas tree fire? Back in 1995?"

"Yeah," said Abe. "We were jumping from the couch to the piano bench, performing our patented version of 'The Twelve Days of Christmas'—you know, the part about the lords a-leaping—and JJ knocked the tree into the fireplace."

Oh, yeah, I thought. *Those* cousins. I'd never met them, but Mom once showed me a picture of three scruffy brothers who had been named after an old song—"Abraham, Martin, and John"—though she referred to them as the Holy Terrors.

Abe, who apparently read my mind, protested. "Holy Terrors? No way. We're not the least bit holy."

"Yeah," said JJ, the little one, whose shaved head resembled a big knuckle. "Now we're known as the Kentucky Fried Children."

That cracked me up. These guys were definitely related to me.

With a big smile, JJ added, "You'd be surprised how fast a Christmas tree can burn down a house."

"I'll bet," I said, remembering the time I dragged one into the backyard and exploded it with a match.

"Anyway," said Marty, "we're your guides. We're your homies away from home." They all grinned.

"Guides? You mean like angels who watch over me and everything?"

"Well," said Abe, putting his arm on my shoulder, "that's the basic idea."

I studied each of them. "But I thought you'd be a lot older. I thought you'd all be wearing these flowing white robes and have these long gray beards."

Marty flipped back his shaggy hair. "That's not exactly our style."

"Speak for yourself," said JJ. The little guy with the buzzed head now sported a two-foot-long beard that hung down to his belt like a bib. "How do I look?"

"Ridiculous," Marty told him. "Which, for you, is an improvement."

"Oh, stick a bowling ball in it, Goldilocks."

"Well, maybe I would," said Marty, "if you weren't using it for a head."

That exchange triggered a small war. They both flew up and lunged for each other, becoming wild-eyed wrestlers, whirling into a tangled mess of hands, feet, and elbows. Very cool.

Then Abe blew right through them, like an asteroid splitting open the moon. "Knock it off, you clowns. What kind of impression do you think you're making on our California cousin? You want him to turn around and leave?"

Leave? I thought. "You mean I could still go back? I thought I was—"

"Well, actually," Abe said, rubbing his long chin, "you're not quite a goner yet. You see, you arrived a little early. And when that happens—"

"What do you mean, early?"

"What he means," said Marty, "is that today was just supposed to be an ordinary day at the ballpark for you. One infield hit, two strikeouts, and a pop-up."

"That figures." Though I loved baseball, I was rather mediocre at it. In fact, even though my whole family loved baseball, none of us were spectacular athletes. What we loved were the strategies of the game and watching the challenges unfold between key players—the dramatic, athletic chess moves. In short, the magic of baseball.

"What he means," said Abe, "is that there were no major life events scheduled for you at all today."

Not a surprise. "Are there ever?"

Marty whapped JJ on his head from behind with what I think was a gong. They both flew off at lightning speed.

"Well, that's beside the point." Abe folded his arms. "But just for the record, what was the last thought you had right before . . . the Big Bang?"

I shrugged. "Nothing much. I was just out there warming up, playing catch, dreaming as usual."

"Dreaming what?"

I tilted my head. "Something like, if only I could, just once, *feel* what it was like to connect with Charlie Musselwhite's mighty bat, I'd die a happy man."

That brought all three of them whooshing up to my ethereal face, inches away. Abe even opened his mouth to talk. "Oh, no. That's what did it."

"You connected all right," said JJ, now holding Marty in a headlock. "Big time."

Oh, man, I thought. Just great. I can't even dream right.

"Don't be too hard on yourself," said Marty, who sent JJ flying backwards with an elbow to his gut. "Dreaming is an art, too, just like baseball."

Suddenly, a long, dark tunnel appeared in front of us.

I'm serious. A tunnel, just like in the movies. Only this one wasn't some long, foggy tube, lined with dark clouds and singing angels and with a bright light at the end. This tunnel was square, with a concrete floor and shiny blue walls and no end in sight. And it smelled like gym class. It smelled like sweat socks.

Abe pointed at Marty and JJ. "Truce, you two! We got work to do." Quietly, as if a ritual had begun, they gathered close and began to guide me into the tunnel.

"Where are we going?"

"We're going," said Marty, "where every baseball player wants to go. Home."

I followed them, though I was fairly confused. "You mean home plate?"

They took turns answering, oldest to youngest, as if reciting a poem.

"Home plate. Home field."

"Home team. Hometown."

"And the *hooome*," sang JJ, "of the *braaave!*"

"Play ball!" they shouted.

I suddenly realized where we were. The concrete walls. The smell of sweat. We were in a locker room tunnel. We were heading to a baseball park!

"Are we going to play baseball?"

"Do pigs fly?" asked JJ.

"Well, not—"

"Up here they do," said Abe, "and at the time we got the Call about you, we were already on our way to a game."

"A game? You guys were going off to play baseball instead of watching over me? Some guides you are."

"But you were supposed to be okay," said Marty.

Abe brightened. "Besides, it was a bodacious game for us. Against the 1927 New York Yankees."

My eyes must've grown as big as the rings of Saturn. "Really? With Babe Ruth and Lou Gehrig and everybody?

You were getting ready to play the most legendary team in baseball history?"

JJ pinched his nose and fanned his face. "Ah, they stink."

"What?"

"We could cream them any day of the week," said Marty, "and twice on sunny days."

"You lie. No way. I mean, *those* guys?"

"Those guys," said Abe, "are not the greatest players in the universe anymore. They're way too busy doing other things."

"Yeah, like visiting sick kids on earth," said JJ. "Or saving puppy dogs from drowning. Goody-goody stuff."

"They're still decent ballplayers," Marty noted, "but they're not as serious about baseball as we are. Shoot, we can score on them at will."

"Yeah," JJ added. "Anytime we want. Run after run. We're so good, we make Derek Jeter look like some ol' Grandma Geezer swinging a parking meter."

"Score at will?" I stared at JJ in disbelief. "That is so hard to believe." He just kept walking and began to juggle three shiny balls while balancing a bat on his nose.

"Well, believe this," said Abe. "You can be as good

as you want to be up here, Peter. And we can show you how."

As he spoke those words, we stepped out of the dark tunnel and into the most beautiful dugout I'd ever seen. Everything from the players' bench to the dugout steps to the bat rack was made of white marble trimmed in rosy quartz.

The field was a lush mystical green garden that had been carved out of a forested mountainside. The air was so light and clear, it seemed like pure oxygen. Lining the ballpark were hundreds of perfect evergreen shrubs, like little Christmas trees, and the fragrance of pine scented the air. In the sky beyond center field were the planets and stars, so big and close that they shined in the daylight.

This was too much. "Wait a minute. I'm starting to go wacko." I looked at the crystalline scoreboard, mounted on huge boulders, with its liquid red and green lights vibrating boldly. I turned back, feeling confused. "There was something I was going to ask you guys. But now I can't even remember."

Marty pulled some gear out of his leopard-skin sports bag. "Maybe it'll come back to you."

"It hardly ever does. I just get so distracted. My dad says I have focus issues." Then suddenly, it did come back. In the far reaches of my mind, a thought crept up, a pang of concern about being here, about leaving my mom and dad, who were probably still driving to the ballpark hoping to catch my game.

"Going back!" I blurted out. "That was it. You guys said I could still go back."

Abe narrowed an eye at me. "Sure, but why would you want to?"

"My parents, for one thing."

They all sent me puzzled looks, as if to say, *"Parents?"*

"Well, you know." I tried to think of a better reason. "They still owe me my allowance. I get seven bucks every Saturday."

"Big whoop," said JJ, who now not only had a bat on his nose, but had also stacked the three baseballs on top.

"And," I added, "my birthday is coming up in a couple of weeks."

What I didn't say was that I hoped my parents would let me have a party so I could invite Lola, so I could finally tell her why I think she is so stellar.

"Lola, is it?" said Marty. "What're you gonna tell her, lover boy?"

Oh, no. I forgot they could hear my thoughts.

"Nothing, just, you know, that I kind of, sort of . . . like her."

Marty swiped the bat off of JJ's nose and hit each ball out onto the field, one by one, as they fell.

Then JJ and Marty joined forces, standing side by side like two doo-wop dorks from the 1950s with slick hair and white shoes.

"*Lola,*" they sang, placing a hand on their hearts, "*you drive me out of controlla! You are my heart and soul-a. If you were a soup, I'd order a bowl-a Lola. Do-wah, do-wah.*"

Abe cut them off. "Guys, quiet." He turned to me. "Let me get this straight, Peter. You want to go back to earth in order to face almost certain rejection by a fourteen-year-old girl who barely knows you exist?"

When I hesitated, JJ piled on. "Could that be true . . . *Flathead?*"

Oh, yeah. That. I reached up and touched my ethereal brow, which of course felt fine. It was the one on earth that had "fracture" issues. How, I wondered, could I possibly approach Lola looking like I do now?

I fell back to the dugout bench. It was a lot to absorb. "So you're saying that I can go, but if I do, I'll be some drooling veggie boy with a cracked skull?"

JJ conjured up a jack-o'-lantern and pulled it over his head. "You got it."

"No, no, no," said Abe, who sat down beside me. "Don't listen to these guys. Here's the deal, Peter. Since what happened today was a spontaneous unplanned cosmic collision—that is, an accident—caused by the caustic combo of two boys trying to impress two different girls while in extremely close proximity, if you decide to go back to your earthly body, you can. Your medical case would then become the sort doctors typically shake their heads at. What people on earth call a miracle."

"Really?" I said. "Me? A miracle boy?"

"Yep, but listen. If you want to go, you better tell us quick, because pretty soon it's gonna be too late."

"How long do I have?"

Abe pointed to home plate. "Till game time. When the umpire yells 'Play ball!' you're either with us or you're going, going, *gone.*"

I scanned the perfect grass, the perfectly smooth red clay base paths, the brilliant white canvas bases. "Was all that other stuff you said true, too? About what kind of player I could be?"

"Absolutely," said Marty. "Up here you can be a better home-run hitter than Hank Aaron and Babe Ruth combined."

"No way!"

"Milky Way!" said JJ. "And we can give you a little taste." He clapped his hands, calling, "Drumroll, please." A snare drum instantly appeared in his grasp. He rolled it across the dugout. After the crash, he announced, "Ladies and gentlemen, boys and squirrels."

"There are no *ladies* here," said Marty.

JJ glared at him. "Bowling ball! Bowling ball! Coming soon to a mouth near you, if you don't shut it." He harrumphed, turned, then began again, in his announcer's voice. "*Imaginary* ladies and gentlemen. Our cousin, Peter, will now join us in a game of red-hot chili pepper to warm up for today's match."

"I will? But I don't think I know how."

Abe patted my back. "We'll show you, bud. Look and learn."

I stepped out of the dugout to watch as my cousins ran into right field and began playing a game of three-man pepper. But it was no ordinary game of two fielders lobbing pitches at a batter who knocked soft rollers back at them. Instead, Abe and Marty stood side by side, about twenty feet away, juggling three balls each, then Hacky-Sacking them one at a time off their shoes, as pitches to JJ.

No matter where the balls were pitched—or rather, kicked—JJ would return them sharply with his bat, like machine-gun bullets, only to have one brother or the other snag the balls and flip them straight up, until they were again juggling three each. Then they'd start all over.

They played like flying circus clowns who could do ten things at once.

As much as I really wanted to play their red-hot brand of pepper, I knew my skill level was nothing like theirs. So I stepped back inside the dugout and sank down onto the bench, filled with a strange mix of disappointment and awe.

Behind me, from out of the mouth of the tunnel burst half a dozen more ballplayers, all dressed like my cousins. They ran onto the field and began their own warm-up drills.

From somewhere down the mountain, out past left field,

I thought I heard a rumble of truck engines, music, and voices. Before long, two flatbed trucks, like from the way olden days, came rolling up out of the trees and onto the meadow just beyond left field.

The long, low truck beds were filled with people— dancers, singers, musicians, *and* baseball players.

I stood for a better look. "Oh, my gosh." The ballplayers wore the classic old woolen pinstripes. I spotted Babe Ruth right off.

"It's them," I whispered. "The 1927 New York Yankees."

The trucks, like two parade floats, rolled to a stop, and the ballplayers jumped off. But the band kept playing, horns and drums, and the dancers spread out into a chorus line of gossamer gowns, using the flatbeds as one big stage.

I spied Lou Gehrig walking through left field. Number 4. His mitt dangled from the barrel of a long white bat propped over his shoulder. Next to him was the great second baseman Tony Lazzeri.

What if I could learn to play ball like these guys? I thought. Wouldn't Lola be amazed? Wouldn't she go crazy?

I darted out to right field. "Look, you guys! The Yankees!"

Marty tossed me his glove. "We know. Twenty minutes to game time, cuz. What're you going to do?"

I slipped Marty's silk-lined glove onto my hand and took my place alongside Abe. "I don't know, but for right now, I'm going to do my best to play some red-hot chili pepper." I could not believe I was sharing a ball field with the awesome '27 Yanks.

Marty flipped me a ball. I caught it with my bare hand and held the glowing orb in my palm. Whoa. I instantly felt my arm becoming stronger, more energized, as if the ball had given me extra power.

JJ stood with his bat pulled back and grinned. "What're you waiting for?"

"Nothing." I squeezed the ball and felt the vibrations of energy surge through every part of me. I shifted it in my hand so that I felt the seams beneath my fingertips. Fastball grip. And though I knew that in pepper a soft toss was more appropriate, I couldn't hold back.

"Here comes!" It was a flamer, the hardest pitch I'd ever thrown.

And he banged it back as easy as a cat swatting a cotton puff.

So what? I fielded it, a sharp one-hopper, smooth as—well, smooth as the silk inside my glove.

I loved how it felt to play with such *electricity*. I was ten times the infielder here that I was on earth. I was ten times the pitcher. I wondered if I could be ten times the hitter—or even half as good as JJ, who kept whacking every ball we threw at him, whether it was behind him, over his head, or on the ground. No matter how ridiculous the pitch, he managed to drive it back to us with ease.

Finally I asked, "How do you keep hitting these crazy pitches?"

"Something I learned from Babe Ruth."

"That's right," said Abe. "He taught all of us how to hit any pitch, in any location, anywhere we wanted it to go."

"It was so cool." Marty smashed a fist into his palm. "The Babe used to stand up at bat and point straight out to the moon. Then he'd smack a ball into it."

"But," said Abe, "he did kinda mess up the moon."

I gave the pockmarked moon a quick glance. "I always wondered why it looked like that. But do you really think I could learn to hit any pitch, any place?"

"I don't see why not," said Abe. "Go on up to bat and give it a try."

I flipped Marty's glove back to him, then jogged up to take a turn hitting. And after only a few pitches, I was socking the ball almost the way JJ had done.

Whoa, I thought, if only Lola could see this. Pitching, fielding, hitting like a superstar. Maybe she'd forget how dumb I looked the last time she saw me.

On and on we played, rotating positions, laughing and joking. About five minutes before game time, I knew one thing for certain.

I wanted to stay here forever.

The rush, the energy, the joy. I'd never felt anything like it in my life.

"Managers!" the umpire called from home plate. "It's time to get rolling."

We looked toward home. The pregame coaches-and-umpires meeting was about to begin.

"So, Petey," said Abe. "What'd you decide? Staying here or going back?"

"I'm staying, you guys. Definitely. I want to play this game."

"Ya-hoo!" they yelled, sending a fireworks display of energy out of their fingertips and into the sky. "We're gonna have so much fun," screamed JJ, firing a loose ball at me.

I caught it with my bare hand and shook it over my head, feeling the energy zing into my arm. "Hey, guys," I said. "One last pitch, okay?"

"Fire away." JJ twirled his bat like a drum major's baton. He flung it up, then caught it in a batter's stance, ready to hit.

I fired away. But this time, I put a little extra zing on the ball. I gave it some *celestial zip,* you might say, trying to throw him an unhittable pitch, just to see if I could.

And I got him! Well, nearly.

He didn't exactly miss the ball, but he *mistimed* it. Popped it straight up. The first one he'd blooped today.

I could've stood there gloating, but it occurred to me that if I started sprinting, I actually had a chance to catch the ball. Wouldn't that be cool? I focused with "intensaroony," which is what Dad calls really paying attention. I used my tunnel vision.

I bolted. I surged. At the last instant, I dove.

Riding my elbows and my knees, I felt the knuckles of my glove scrape against the grass as I stretched to my fullest reach. And just before it hit the field, I snagged that ball in the tip of my glove.

Wow. Perfect catch. It was the kind of spectacular catch I never could have made before today. The kind of miracle catch I wanted to make on the high toss from Speedy. The kind I wanted Lola to see.

And in the split second it took for me to come to a sliding stop at JJ's feet, I realized I'd made a huge mistake. In that instant I realized that no matter how good I was now, how great my skills, Lola would never—no one on earth would ever—see me make a catch like this. This place will always be here, I decided, but I would not always be with my friends and family on earth.

I wished I had not chosen to stay.

As I lay at JJ's feet, I noticed his front foot shift a bit the way a batter does as he steps forward to swing at the ball.

Stop, JJ! Didn't he see the ball in my glove? Was he nuts? Apparently so.

JJ swung, but this time he missed the ball. He even missed my glove. He did not, however, miss my head.

In the next instant, I felt myself moving back rapidly, zooming into the dugout feet first, then down the tunnel, as though I were Superman flying backwards, being sucked into some vortex.

I woke up in a hospital bed. I was staring at the ceiling instead of floating up there and looking down. I was back—sent back by a quick-thinking mind-reading cousin who knew I had made a mistake and my time was running out.

Mom was the first to notice. "He opened his eyes!"

My dad appeared, gazing down. "Peter, can you hear me?"

I blinked. My throat was dry and sore. I wished I could talk using only my mind, but I did manage to gasp out a crackling, "Yeah."

They both started crying. Oh, man. Major waterworks. It was embarrassing. I wanted to tell them to stop, to tell them all about what I'd seen and everything I'd just been through, but I had so little strength. I must have fallen back to sleep, because when I woke up the next time, there were a lot more people in the room.

A doctor, two nurses, Charlie, Mandy, Lola, Speedy, and my coach. And more. Behind that crowd stood—bigger than life—the Kentucky Fried Idiots.

"What're you guys doing here?" I blurted out.

Mom answered. "We never left your side, honey. We've been here all night."

"No," I said, trying to motion at my cousins with my eyes. "Those guys."

"Put a bowling ball in it," said JJ, now showing me a goofy, toothless grin. "They can't see us."

Mom looked around at Charlie and the gang, saying, "They're here to be with you."

"And," said Marty, "we're here to make sure you didn't get lost on the way home."

Abe sidled in between his brothers. "What these two *stupidos* and I really want to say is that we'll be sure to be around from now on. Whenever you need us."

"Cool. Thanks, guys," I said.

Everyone—the humans, anyway—laughed.

For some reason, my eyes found Lola's, as if I were no longer afraid of her. She seemed to sense it, too.

"I was so worried," she said. "I'm glad you didn't—I mean, I'm so glad you woke up." She smiled shyly, unsure of herself, glancing down at her hands, then back at me, adding, "I really wanted you to be okay."

For an instant, it was as if she and I were the only people in the room. But only for an instant. Because then my cousins began to echo her sentiment.

"Yeah, Petey, sweetie," they sang in syrupy singsong voices. "She really *wanted* you."

They spun around, like blades on a propeller, crossing their eyes and sticking out their tongues and pulling away, shrinking to the back of the room. As much as those goof-balls drove me crazy, I was afraid they'd just leave, so I called out to them. "Look, I don't care how stupid you act. I think you're awesome."

Lola's eyes grew wide. "What?"

I blinked back to Lola. "What? No, I mean . . ."

"Yeah," said JJ. "What *did* you mean, *lover boy*?"

"Oh, be quiet," I said.

"Peter!" Mom was trying to save me. She turned to Lola. "He's not himself right now."

The doctor cleared his throat, as if deciding to change the subject. "I still cannot get over these X-rays." He glanced at a light box on the wall. "They show signs of spontaneous mending along the fracture lines." He looked back at me. "Swelling is down, too. It's something I've never seen before."

"It's a *mir-uh-cull*!" my cousins sang again.

I laughed. What else could I do?

"Hey," said Abe. "Before we fade away, there's someone else here who wants to see you."

My cousins shifted apart, and from between them appeared the great Sultan of Swat himself, Babe Ruth.

"Rough day, eh, kid?" he said, as if he knew all about it. "How ya doin'?"

Holy cow. *This* was a miracle. "I think I'll make it."

The doctor smiled. "Well, good. I like your attitude, son." He put his stethoscope to his ears, then leaned in to listen to my chest.

We—Babe Ruth and I—ignored the doctor and kept talking.

"Always remember the lesson you learned today," the Babe said. "When in doubt, follow your heart."

"Maybe I should go," said Lola.

"Okay, Babe," I told him. "But watch out for those clowns behind you. They think they can score on you anytime they want."

"Peter!" Mom called with shock in her voice. She put a hand to her mouth.

"I'm so sorry," Dad said to Lola. "He didn't mean—"

Lola only laughed. Turning to Charlie and Speedy and

giving them a stern glare, she said, "Thanks for the good advice, Peter. Nice to know someone cares."

"Ah," said Marty. "Our work here is done."

The Babe winked, then began to fade. My cousins too.

They all sent me a wave, and all four of them were gone.

For the Love of Pork

By

Jack Gantos

I really want to tell you something funny about how my family and I get along, but first I have to tell you how we don't. We are the kind of rigid, pigheaded people who would never change our totally annoying behavior for anyone. We do not practice what we consider to be the vile, compromising "give-and-take" method of family harmony. None of that weak "smoothing things over" granny crap for us. We either give, give, and give or take, take, and take. But we don't do both at the same time.

The only truly refined feature we have as a family is that, despite our stubborn, hard-nosed qualities, we boldly practice unconditional love. This means that we may despise everything you do and say and wear and eat and stand for, but we will love you anyway. We kiss, we hug, we embrace, and we stomp off in a snit—then we return and do it all over again. This may sound twisted, but we have found this love-hate-love-hate-love cycle to be the only way to (a) allow everyone to be totally themselves even if we can't stand them and (b) allow everyone to be loved regardless of our snotty judgmental opinions.

This high-stakes combo of undiluted loathing and unconditional love might cause you to think that our strident personal traits create nonstop angst, hatred, fear, grief, hand-wringing, disgust, and murderous thoughts toward each other. Well, it does—but only for a while because the unconditional love has a way of taking the most wicked of intentions and twisting them into some sort of surreal quixotic humor—which is where this little family story begins.

So let me introduce the cast (there are only three of us). There is me (Joshua), my mother, and my father, who is a preacher—and I mean the kind of preacher who *can't stop preaching*. It's like his mouth is on fire with the hot colonic peppers of biblical hell and damnation. God, he's really hard to live with, and I would have gladly gone off to live with my mom after she left him because I love her, too, but I have some special needs that her New Jersey vegan boyfriend could not accept. I really have a thing for pork and couldn't possibly give it up (no, I do NOT think this is a shallow trait). I mean, as much as Dad likes biblical perfection, I like pork—chops, sausages, rinds, barbecue ribs, bacon, and those little jars of bacon bits. Man, that's good eating. As far as I'm concerned all food should taste like pork. It is the *perfect* flavor: salty, greasy, and with a porcine musk that is like the call of the wild to pork lovers everywhere. I eat a pork product at least once a day. Each juicy bite is like a little bit of love in my tummy, and that keeps me happy— and who knows, maybe that pork-driven happiness is what gives me the strength to shower my parents with unconditional love.

I'll get to my mom and her boyfriend in a moment, but stick with me while I talk about Dad. He did a lot of stupid religious preaching in public parks and bus stations and outside of liquor stores, but it was after the ugly "intelligent design" theory incident at school things really started to fall apart. He came to my science class and threatened the science teacher with "eternal damnation" if he ever dared to teach Darwin's "fictional theory of evolution." Naturally you can't just go around threatening teachers, so the police were called. I heard my father shouting as they dragged him down the hallway toward the exit, "My mouth is a weapon of God, and I'm cocked and locked. I'm armed and dangerous."

He's dangerous, all right. Nobody is disputing that theory.

It was right after that ugly episode that Mom went to her doctor and got Dad some special medication to even out his moods, but he wasn't good at taking the happy pills. She put her foot down and told him if he didn't start taking the medication to control his public outbursts, she would leave him. "I love you," she said, clutching her heart. "God knows I do. But even with my immense love for you, I'm getting to the point where I may snap and kill you, and that would be unforgivable. So take the pills or I'm outta here before I have blood on my hands."

As she pointed toward the front door with an "I mean

it" expression on her face, he very deliberately dropped the medication—little orange plastic bottle and all—into the blender on the kitchen counter and turned it on. That made quite a racket. When he turned off the blender, he declared, "Medication is against my religious beliefs."

Her eyes bugged out. "Well, as of this day, continuing to live with a holy maniac is against my beliefs," Mom declared right back, then marched into the bedroom and packed her bags.

"I love him," she responded when I reminded her about our family's unconditional love rule. "But sometimes I think your father made that rule up to keep me from strangling him."

"But it's a good rule," I said, trying to calm her down. "It encourages forgiveness, and we have always agreed that there is nothing more important than forgiveness. Besides, I'll be really hurt if you run off on me."

"You'll forgive me for that," she said, dumping an entire drawer of jewelry into her openmouthed handbag. "He'll drive you nuts, too. Sooner or later he'll get to you and your reserve of unconditional love will dry up and you'll come find me before you reach for a kitchen knife and do him in. Mark my words."

And off she went on her own. She was always the brave one in the family.

"She'll regret this," Dad said the moment the door slammed. "She loves me way too much to let her anger cloud her vision. She'll be back. She's a lover, not a leaver." Then he returned to wrapping used Bibles with baling wire to create what he called "God's bricks of love," which he heaved at porn shop windows while I drove a rental car with my football helmet on.

Of course Mom still loved him, but she must have gone around the bend because before too long she was living with the New Jersey vegan who reeked of so much Tiger Balm it made your eyes water to get near him. She claimed he was refreshingly liberal and didn't pick on her constantly for every little thing she would do or say. She said that living with the vegan was like losing "a hundred pounds of fatty insults your father had packed around my hips." I have a very visual imagination and wish she hadn't said that.

She had met the New Jersey vegan at a group therapy session that helped people get over their "loss." Mom had lost Dad to excessive nasty preaching, and the vegan's wife had slipped on the ice and hit her head and passed away. Even though it was a real vegetarian-banana-peel sort of death, it was still quite sad. The vegan was a good guy, despite the Tiger Balm and that funky Gandhi diaper he liked to wear while grocery shopping. If I brought up the joys of eating pork to him, he could get a tirade launched about the crime against nature of eating animals, but he was in a Single-A Preaching League compared to Dad, who is a Big-League All-Star preacher and the number-one soul-saver on God's team. He even calls himself a *closer*.

"When a person's faith is on the line, call me in!" he brags. "I'll strike out their doubts and chalk up another save for Christ."

I call him "mini God," but only behind his back because he has no sense of humor. If I called him "mini God" to his face, he'd go ballistic and call me a bunch of stupid biblical slurs as if quoting from some potty-mouthed version of the Bible.

And I'm not allowed to make fun of how he looks, either. He's built like a bowlegged twinkle-eyed leprechaun with a mouth the size of a toothless T. rex. He used to have caveman-sized teeth, but after he called that big guy at the Planned Parenthood march a baby-killer, the guy punched him so hard he spun around and hit a parking meter and knocked his teeth out. Later he told me that punch was like "an Old Testament test. You know, where the old-timey gods really put the pain to you in order to test your love of the one true God."

"I guess," I replied. What else could I say? I loved him. He was my dad, teeth or no teeth. In a way, he was my test.

Outside of not having dental insurance, he's got a lot of problems, but I've boiled them all down to one tidy little problem—that is, he is one of those guys who always talks about how the world "should be." It should be more "respectful," and more "God worshiping," and more "grace driven." The usual "should be" stuff. This basically means he is in love with perfection *according to him.* The truth of a situation—hard-core reality—means nothing compared to what the *truth should be.*

Take, for example, the guy who punched him in the face. Instead of Dad realizing that he offended the guy and as a result got popped in the face, he says Planned Parenthood supporters have "psychological problems" and "anger issues" and "not enough love in their hearts." Once he makes up his mind about something, there is no arguing him away from his point of view, so I just have to put up with him.

I forgave my mom for running off and I miss her and wish I could visit her more, but it's hard for me. I mean if you have one bit of aromatic bacon between your teeth, an ANIMAL EATER! alarm will sound when you pass over his threshold. The vegan is a gentle guy and he is nice to my mom and she is happy so I don't like to complain one little bit about him, but of all his food restrictions he has no humor when it comes to the pig. One oink and you are boiled in oil. Once he made a really good joke about Jews, Christians, and Muslims in heaven and they met God and so on and so forth, and the punch line was wicked clever and I gave one of those nose-snorting laughs and, you know, really oink-oink-oinked a good one, and he asked me if I was being disrespectful. I said, "No, it was just a good laugh," and he said he thought I was making pig sounds on purpose and asked me to leave the house. My mom shrugged. "Don't take it personally," she said. "He's from New Jersey. He has to have something to complain about."

By the time I passed beyond his front door I had forgiven him. No big deal. Besides, I was getting a little hungry for a pork sausage and pepper sub with cheese fries.

To tell the truth, I *was* making intentional pig-oinking

laughter. I can be a jerk, and I'm a little stupid, too, because Dad said it was okay for me not to go to school anymore because of the "evolution propaganda." That is another reason why I like staying with him. The rules of life mean *nothing* to him. Laws mean *nothing* to him. Manners mean *nothing* to him. Doing what is on his mind and saying what is in his mouth is what matters to him. I could tolerate all of that and more, but then we started to become poor and porkless, and being porkless was putting a hurt on me.

The reason my dad is out of work is because he was booted out of his own church for intolerance. He is an Episcopalian preacher, and when the Episcopalians chose a gay preacher for their new bishop, Dad went ballistic. But the congregation was fine with the new gay bishop, and after being patient with Dad's nasty attitude for a while, they got fed up and voted him out. He was fired. I mean, that is bad when you get kicked out of a church. So he started preaching to me against gays and the new "gay-loving church." After a few days of his nonstop tirades, I thought I'd actually give up bacon and fried fatback sandwiches to go live with my mom, wear a diaper, and eat vegetarian pap. But that great belief in unconditional love keeps Dad and me together in good times and bad.

Well, I take that back. When times are bad, unconditional love seems a lot less important because without
money you don't have perfection or pork. You have poverty
and pasta and rice and potatoes. He and I were both against
that evil veganlike situation. You can't eat the Bible, and I
had polished off my last jar of bacon bits and was reduced
to eating from a pouch of old beef jerky I found in a cup-
board. I think that jerky may have belonged to the last
owner of the house because each piece was as hard and
sharp as an Indian arrowhead. I was on the last of it when
I said to him, "You are the dad. Go get a job. I mean, I can't
believe I'm reduced to eating beef darts."

"So stop eating them," he said. "Besides, that stuff looks
like old scabs."

"Go make money," I said. "I'm starving."

"You're right," he replied, and seemed contrite that he
was letting me down. "It's time for me to find people who
think like me."

Or people who can just tolerate you, I thought, knowing
better than to say it out loud.

He stood up, went into his bedroom and put on his
preacher robes, then walked out the front door. I figured he
would be going from church to church pounding on those

medieval-style doors and asking for work. I hoped someone would hire him because I've never been a beef eater, and I sure didn't want to sink so low that I would eat a piece of chicken. I've never eaten a bird. They can't even make jerky out of birds. And putting chicken on a barbecue grill is just a sin because it takes up the space where pork should be sizzling.

That night when Dad came home, I asked if he got a job.

"Hell, no," he said, and tossed the classified ads onto the couch. "Damn religious people are all hypocrites. I told them I was perfect for the job. They kept asking me what I thought my flaws were. I told them I don't have any damn flaws. They want everyone to be equally messed up so they can *relate* and *save* you. Well, I'm tired of that nonsense. I don't need to be saved—I need to go out into the world and save others 'cause there is no *true* saving going on in the church!"

I was thinking that I wish someone would save me a piece of pork loaf. I swear I smelled one baking down the street.

"But," Dad continued, "I stumbled upon a new church with a lot of financial potential. Kind of a new age cathe-

dral," he added. "I'm going to deliver a service there tomorrow. I'll need you to pass the basket."

"Can I have a few bucks?" I asked. I'll do anything for a
bag of deep-fried pork rinds.

"I'll give you ten percent of the take," he replied. "But be
warned. Ten percent of nothing is nothing."

The next day we woke up at the crack of dawn. He put
his preaching robes on, and I put on some old school
clothes, which were a bit baggy because I had lost weight
from my lack of pork. I looked in the mirror, and I did not
feel thin or trim or buff or agile and athletic. I felt deprived.
"I need pork," I whispered to myself, then joined up with
Dad and went outside and caught the bus.

When we got off the bus, we walked across a vast asphalt
parking lot that was mostly empty. "Why are we at the
mall?" I asked, pointing toward a long white building with
a Sears at one end and a Target at the other.

"Think of the mall as a modern cathedral," Dad said,
with a little twinkle in his eye. "It is three stories high, has
a cathedral ceiling with tall windows, and has a fountain
for a baptismal font, a player piano for the choir, and a
balcony on the second floor from which I can sermonize."

"Maybe you should take your medication," I suggested. "It's still in the blender, and we can pick out the plastic shards."

"This is better than medication," he replied. "It's an opportunity to make some money, and the Lord helps those who help themselves and saves souls on the side."

We walked to the back entrance and waited with a bunch of old people in white sneakers and matching red and blue jogging clothes who were leaning against the white pillars while stretching out their calf muscles. They had been dropped off by their retirement home bus to get some indoor exercise. "See those mall walkers?" Dad whispered. "I'm going to save them, and in return they are going to save us."

Then he moved in among them. "Hello, friends," he said in a heavenly smooth voice. "The first service is at nine fifteen."

"It was nice meeting you yesterday," said a lady who was about seventy-five.

"And you too," Dad replied. "Don't forget, we have communion this morning."

"I haven't forgotten," she said. "We all look forward to it."

"Tomorrow we'll have the washing of the sneakers," he said.

"I'll buy some new ones for the occasion," she replied sweetly. "They'll be clean."

At that moment a smiling security guard opened the door. He seemed to know all the mall walkers. "Good morning, you old hot rods," he said grandly. "Now let's knock some rust off of you so you can get down on the floor and wrestle with your grandchildren."

They wished him a good morning, then lowered their heads, revved their arms back and forth, and took off speed walking down the first floor. They were impressively fast.

"Follow me," Dad said. We walked over to the donut shop, and with a handful of change he bought a box of plain donut holes and grabbed a few empty paper cups.

"I thought we were broke?"

"Manna from heaven," he replied, nodding toward the fountain. Then he pushed me aside on his way toward the steps to the second floor. At that moment the Muzak came on and the fountain began to burble up. As Dad climbed the stairs, the old folks whizzed by. A moment later they were followed by a line of determined moms pushing baby strollers. Behind them were three dangerously obese people, and behind them were really old folks who had those aluminum walkers on wheels, and bringing up the rear were people recovering from strokes and just getting their gait back. In all there were close to fifty people.

"Lap number one," shouted the last guy to drag himself past us. He must have been a gym teacher about a hundred years ago.

After the fifth lap, Dad was ready. He raised his arms and spoke loudly. "Let us all gather and say the Lord's Prayer." I stood by the piano holding the empty cups in my hand as the mall-walking congregation gathered. I figured security would give him the boot, but the guard was right there with us, smiling and praying. Dad said a few beautiful words about how religion doesn't need a church to create a community. He pointed out how all of us had arrived at this same mall for different reasons but had found grace in our common Christian faith. He even allowed me to play "Onward, Christian Soldiers" on the piano, which showed off his lovely baritone voice. Wisely, Dad didn't waste time and soon blessed the donut holes and gave out communion. In the end everyone seemed spiritually satisfied and our cups were full of change and dollar bills.

"See you next week," Dad said. "Go forth in your faith."

On the way home I counted the money. "That was a generous offering," I said to him.

"I've learned something," he replied. "When you tell everyone they are good enough to float up to heaven, they empty their pockets of the dirty ballast of money."

"In other words," I said to him, "you've changed your tune and discovered that being nice to people makes them nice in return."

"Something like that," he replied, not willing to admit he might have adjusted his thinking. And I didn't want to rub it in, because this one small step might lead to other small steps, and who knows, he might be a little easier to live with.

As a result of his newfound tolerance, word of his mall preaching spread, and within weeks people started to show up just to see him. They loved him. And he loved them right back. Sure, they had money, but I could tell it was more than that. And it was not just the old joggers and new moms and obese folks but all kinds of people, including some of the mall workers. Even though a few of the businesses thought it was odd to have a church service in a public place, they let him continue because he actually brought customers to the mall. He was good for business—especially on days when he blessed shoes, elbow pads, bunion softeners, hearing aids, Metamucil, pet products, baby pacifiers— well, just about everything the mall sold he would bless, so he was saving their bottom line. Let's face it—it is a lot easier to tolerate someone when they make money for you.

And once he became nice, he didn't stop there. He kept becoming nicer, and nicer. He was on a roll. His whole "perfection" obsession seemed to pass the more he was away from the church and in the mall. And instead of walking around being grouchy with people and telling them they were going to burn in hell, he switched over to doing good deeds. He began to visit some of the old folks in their nursing homes if they were feeling poorly and couldn't make it to the mall. He performed CPR on a man who collapsed while mall walking and saved his life. He baptized a baby in the fountain. When the security guard caught a shoplifter, Dad advised forgiveness and the guard let him go. He ran evening Bible classes in the Food Court.

And then he shocked me. We were on the bus home from

the mall on a Sunday, and he looked me in the eye. "I'm only going to say this once," he said very seriously. "But I've changed a lot lately because I've discovered that *embracing reality* is the new perfection—once I accepted all those old and infirm people, I was the one who ended up feeling perfect. Loving *them* made *me* feel better."

Yeah, I know that sounds sort of trite and maybe he should have figured this out a long time ago, but I love him for finally getting to the point that religion shouldn't be about fear. Right? It should be about making you feel great, even if you are not.

"But I have more to tell you," he added.

Don't push it, I thought. We are in a really good place at the moment.

"Now that I'm in love with reality, I miss your mom," he declared. "And even you don't drive me as nuts as you usually do. Sure, it hurts me that you don't go to school and that you have become really stupid. Believe me, it is hard to forgive people who are intentionally stupid—but for you, I will try to accept and forgive your stupidity."

"Thanks," I said, and smiled at him, but it was a fake smile because I wanted to kill him. I guess my unconditional love for him had switched over into the contempt portion of the love cycle.

And thank God Mom's love cycle had turned back the other way. One morning I was pounding out "Rock of Ages" on the piano when she walked right into the church part of the mall, and when I passed the basket her way, she put a note in it. After the basket returned to me, I opened the note.

"Forgive me," it read. Right away I got tears in my eyes, and when I looked up from the note, she waved to me. I went over and gave her a kiss.

"Things must be going well," she remarked. "There is pork on your breath."

"Where's the vegan?" I asked, and looked around. I figured if Dad saw him, he'd go ballistic and ruin our new gig.

"The vegan was the nicest guy in the world," she explained, "but sadly he never could get over his former wife, so he thought he shouldn't put his sadness on me for the rest of my life."

"Reality is the hardest reality to accept," I said wisely, stressing each word as if I were Buddha.

She frowned. "Yeah, one hand clapping or whatever," she said dismissively. "So I said to the vegan, 'Don't be sad, just be in love with her memory.' But he was clinging to his own sadness and couldn't let it go. And before long his sadness wore off on me, and I began to miss clinging to your father."

"The vegan really is a decent guy," I said, and put my arm around her. "He's tragic, but decent." Privately I thought that without pork, he and I never had a future.

Of course Dad embraced the reality of Mom's return and instantly took her back. Their mutual forgiveness cancelled out all the bad stuff, and it was as if nothing mean and ugly had ever happened. They held hands and kept kissing on the bus, which was a reality that made me sort of sick.

"Could you not do that in public?" I asked.

"You are so jealous," Dad replied. "You need to go back to school and get your own girlfriend."

I'm not too stupid to do that, I thought.

The first thing Mom did when we got home was to clean out the blender. "You didn't need meds after all," she said over the sound of the garbage disposal. "You just needed to do something good for other people and then you fell in love with them, then you fell in love with yourself, then you were ready to fall in love with me. That's how it works."

"I did fall in love with them," he said, rubbing the side of his head like a confused caveman. "And once that happened, I was so happy because I could give up all that 'you have to be perfect' crap and just love everyone and everything for exactly what it is."

She turned her head toward me so I could see her eyes roll. "Sooner or later," she groaned, "everyone figures out that unconditional love is the special sauce on reality, so welcome to the club."

He grinned and walked over to her for a hug. But she had had enough of the mushy stuff. Instead, she plucked a couple really long, thick, nasty white hairs from his eyebrows.

"Does that make me look better?" he asked, rubbing his eyebrows.

"No," she replied. "You will always look like a beakless rooster. If love was about looks, I'd be long gone. I'm with you because loving you makes me happy, and I like being happy."

He began to say something when she gave him a warning look and said, "Don't ruin it for me." He seemed to get what she was saying, so he zippered his lips and just grinned.

In the meantime, I counted up our savings, which were

considerable. I mean I could have bought a lot of pork products. I could have bought a whole pig, but because I really loved him, I figured I could slow down on the pork and we could save to buy him some new teeth.

"Hey, Dad," I said as I sorted the cash into little piles.

"Yeah?" he replied.

"If you think about being a jerk and getting fired from the church and losing Mom and almost going broke and then figuring out a new way to make money by becoming a better person and getting Mom back, you could actually conclude that you have *evolved*. Like, you are the living spirit of Darwin's *theory of evolution*."

He looked up at the ceiling. He rubbed his jaw. Then he looked at me. "And you," he said, "are the poster child for devolution. You haven't changed your porkish ways one bit."

"Yes, he has," Mom piped in. "He'll be going back to school tomorrow, and I'm packing him a vegetarian lunch."

Of course my jaw dropped when she said the word *vegetarian*, but to tell you the truth, it was my turn to do some changing, and I was ready. Besides, I mean, have you ever seen how they kill a pig? They have to do it quickly because the look in the pig's eye just says, "I love you. I love you unconditionally. Please don't eat me. I'll be your piggy friend forever if you spare my life."

I mean, once you realize pigs don't want to be eaten any more than you do, there is nothing left to do but change. So I'm off pork. The pig thing is over. I'd rather a pig live a long life than die for me. That is the power of love.

Another Chance

By
Sharon Dennis Wyeth

"Marlene Douglas to Mrs. Lamb's office!

"Marlene Douglas to the assistant principal—"

Marli's head jerked as her name blared over the loud-speaker. What the heck did Lamb want now? Probably about the detention she'd skipped the day before. It wasn't like she didn't have an excuse with her asthma. In a high school the size of Harter, you'd think the assistant principal would have more to do than check up on her every move. Not that she minded that much, taking a break from geometry.

A screech came over the PA system as the secretary's voice repeated the page: "Marlene Douglas to—"

Feeling the eyes of the classroom, Marli slammed her notebook and grabbed her knapsack. Just outside the window, a perfect day was waiting. On days like this when Marli was younger, her family would take a trip downtown to see the cherry blossoms. It was bad enough being stuck in school without having your name blared out.

"I don't like this," Mr. Hawthorne grumbled, motioning her to the front. "You can't afford to miss class."

From the corner of the room, Antonia Perkins giggled. Marli snapped her eyes in the nerdy girl's direction; Antonia instantly dropped her smirk. She might be a genius at math, but she was no match for Marli outside the classroom. Not that Marli got into fights, except once in her freshman year when she was forced to. People just knew not to mess with her because of the way she carried herself, the way she walked in the hallways with her eyes straight ahead and face betraying nothing, as if nothing mattered that much. It was something Marli had studied in older girls she respected.

Mr. Hawthorne cleared his throat.

"Did you copy the homework assignment?"

Marli shrugged.

"Is that a yes or a no?"

"Yes," she murmured.

"I'll be on the homework line this evening," Hawthorne offered, "if you need any extra help."

Marli turned away. She secretly liked the skinny young teacher, liked how patient he was when she made a mistake. She knew she should thank him for offering to help, but that wouldn't fit her tough-girl image.

Outside the classroom, Marli sized up the corridor—not too much traffic. In no hurry for the meeting with Lamb, she lingered for a moment, resting against the wall. Lately Ma had been working the late shift at the restaurant, so Marli felt tired. She found it hard to fall asleep until Ma got home, a habit left over from the days when she babysat her brother. Now Kyle was almost fourteen and a freshman himself at Harter. Marli was only two years older, but to her, Kyle would always be the baby of the family.

Thinking of Kyle as she strode down the hallway, a nursery rhyme entered her mind, a song the two of them sang when they were little, to the tune of "London Bridge." First they'd sing it with Marli's name, and then with Kyle's, while dancing in a circle:

Marli Lou is falling down,

Falling down, falling down.

Marli Lou is falling down,

Poor, poor Marli. . . .

Marli clicked the song off in her mind; it hurt to think about. They had sung it in the days when Dad lived with them. . . .

Picking up her pace, she straightened her shoulders. Mrs. Lamb was walking toward her.

"There you are, Marlene. Thought you might have gotten lost."

"I missed detention yesterday because of breathing problems," Marli launched in, rapid-fire. "The nurse sent me home. You can check at her office."

Lamb nodded. "And how are you today?" Her wrinkled face was stern, but her eyes were kind.

"Fine. I have a new inhaler."

"Let's go," Lamb said. "Your brother's waiting."

Marli's eyes flew open. "Did Kyle get jumped again?"

"Nothing like that," Lamb assured her.

"Glad to hear it," she quipped, covering her panic. "Kyle's such a crybaby. It's his own fault his arm got broken. He's the one who fell down."

Lamb looked at her oddly. "Those boys took your brother's wallet. Kyle fell down while he was running away. It's perfectly normal that he was scared and upset."

Marli lowered her eyes. She knew that Lamb was right. She'd been really upset herself when Kyle was jumped outside the school. The boys who did it weren't Harter students at all; they were a bunch of dropouts. Maybe if she had been with Kyle, she could have stopped it from happening. Then again, probably not . . . Some people out there were tougher than she was. Marli knew that.

Kyle paced outside Lamb's office. Though he towered over his sister in height, his innocent face made him look young for his age. The cast on his left arm was covered with graffiti.

"What's up?" Marli greeted her brother. "You in trouble?"

Kyle blinked. "Mrs. Lamb didn't tell you?"

"I thought I'd let your mother explain," Lamb interjected.

"Explain what?" Marli wanted to know. "My mother's at work. What's she got to do with it?"

"Ma isn't at work," Kyle said. "I saw her just a minute ago, when she came inside to look for us. She's waiting in the car."

Marli swallowed. Something in Kyle's face made her nervous. "What's going on?" she demanded.

"Ma got a call from Aunt Dee Dee," Kyle said. "Dad's in the hospital."

At the mention of Aunt Dee Dee, Marli felt a pang. When she was younger, Aunt Dee Dee had been her favorite aunt. But because she was Dad's sister, they rarely saw her. Marli and Kyle had lost more than Dad after the divorce.

"Your mother is here to take you to see him," Lamb added gently.

Marli's stomach lurched. They hadn't seen or heard from Dad in five whole years. She chuckled to hide her shock. "Dad? That's a laugh."

"Come on," Kyle coaxed her. "We're keeping Ma waiting."

Behind the wheel of the rickety Ford, Ma had on her waitress uniform; her wispy hair was sticking out from her cap. In the pictures from the time when Marli and Kyle were little, Ma had been beautiful. But these days, Marli thought, she always looked worried and tired; probably from working so hard and trying to make ends meet.

On the ride to the hospital, Marli sat quietly. But Kyle was full of questions.

"When did he have his heart attack?"

"Yesterday," Ma answered.

"Why didn't Aunt Dee Dee call us right away?"

"Guess she figured it was your father's choice, whether he wanted you to know."

"I'm glad Dad told her to call us," Kyle said eagerly.

"About time," Marli snarled. "It's been five years."

Kyle sighed from his seat in the back. "Is Dad going to die?"

Marli clenched her jaw. "Why do you care? He doesn't care about us."

Ma shot her a glance. "Sweetheart, your father still cares about you. You're his children."

"I can't believe you're saying that, Ma," Marli sputtered, "after the way he left us."

Kyle tapped the back of her seat with his foot. "Ma kicked him out. Don't you remember?"

"I'm surprised that you do," Marli said, glancing backward. "I'm surprised you remember Dad at all."

"Yeah," said Kyle. "I remember."

A wave of hurt filled Marli's chest. For years and years, all she'd hoped for was to see Dad again, or to get a call. Then one day she had to stop hoping for something she'd never get. "Dad doesn't even know what I look like," Marli said. "After he left, he forgot all about us."

"Even so," Kyle added wistfully, "I really want to see him again."

"Well, I don't," said Marli. "I don't care if he did have a heart attack."

Ma shot her a glance. "It's up to you, sweetheart. I just thought I'd give you the chance."

At General Hospital, Marli and Kyle waited in the crowded lobby while Ma got passes at the desk. Marli noticed a couple of people being pushed in wheelchairs toward the exit, surrounded by what looked like family. They'd been sick, too, Marli thought nervously, but now they were well. Maybe Dad would get well, too. In the car, Marli had pretended not to care. But she did. Still, that didn't mean she wanted to see him.

"He's in ICU," Ma announced. "But he's in stable condition."

"What's ICU stand for?" Kyle asked.

"Intensive care unit," Ma explained, herding them through the lobby. The elevator doors opened, and the three of them stepped in. Marli had come to General before, but to the emergency room. She'd been sick herself that time with an attack of asthma. But after a shot, she'd felt all right. General was one of the best hospitals in Washington, D.C.

She nudged her mother. "What kind of operation is Dad having?"

"I think a bypass," she answered. "Your Aunt Dee Dee didn't tell me much."

Marli sat in a corner near the nurses' station, while Kyle went in to see Dad. Ma had gone to the cafeteria to get them some hot chocolate. Dad's room was third on the left.

Marli kept her eyes on the door. Part of her wanted to go inside; it had been so long since she'd seen him. But Dad had made her really angry. Marli was scared, too, of seeing Dad while he was sick. She was scared that he might die. She was the big sister in the family; she tried to be tough. But today, Kyle was the brave one. He'd gone into Dad's room not knowing what he would see or what Dad might say.

What if Dad does die? Marli thought. If she didn't visit him now, she might not have another chance. Her chest began to tighten. Retrieving her asthma inhaler from her knapsack, she took a couple of puffs. The last thing she needed was an attack.

The door to Dad's room opened and Kyle ducked out. Marli walked over to meet him.

"How's Dad? Is he really bad off?"

Kyle wrinkled his forehead. "He has a needle with a tube in his arm. Other than that, he looks almost the way I remember." He squeezed Marli's hand. "Dad really wants to see you. He told me to tell you that."

Marli's body trembled. She took a deep breath. The

wheezing she had felt before had gone away. "Okay," she said.

There were two beds in the hospital room, with a partition between them. Marli caught sight of Dad in the one on the right. Like Kyle, Marli thought he looked practically the same, except for a big bald patch in the midst of his curly hair.

Dad's eyes glistened as Marli walked closer.

"It's my little Marli Lou, all grown up," said Dad. "Thanks for coming to see me, honey."

At a loss for words, Marli stood there staring. "You're going bald," she choked.

Dad laughed.

"How are you?" Marli added.

"The doctors say I'll live," Dad reported. "Can't kill a cuss like me."

"Are you sure?" she asked, perching on the edge of the bed. "You're having an operation."

"People have them all the time," he said. "I'll have to learn to take better care of my ticker, change some of my habits. But I'll be okay."

Marli let out a breath. "When Ma said you wanted to see us, I thought maybe it was worse."

"I wanted to see you and Kyle because I have some things to tell you," Dad said, reaching for her hand.

Marli jerked away. "What's there to say? We haven't seen each other for five years."

"And I'm so sorry about that."

A single tear splashed her cheek. She bit her lip to keep from crying.

"I was a terrible father," Dad went on. "Part of it was because I was an alcoholic. But for the past couple of years, I stopped drinking. I'm trying to change. In some ways, I think I have."

Marli got up and walked to the window. Hurt and anger boiled up inside her.

"I just want to explain," he continued, "but if you don't want to—"

"How could you do it, Dad?" she challenged, turning to face him. "How could you just forget about Kyle and me?"

"I didn't, Marli, I promise. I wanted to be in touch, but I'd caused your mother so much pain. The time was never right. I wanted to get myself straight so I could make up—"

He began coughing. Marli swallowed her anger. This wasn't the time. She got Dad a drink from a pitcher on the nightstand. He gulped the water, calming his cough down.

"It's okay, Dad," she said, changing her tone. "We don't have to talk. You're sick."

"I am tired," he admitted. "We can go into all this the next time. . . ."

Marli glanced at him. Would there be a next time? she wondered. Maybe Dad would get worse. Or maybe he wouldn't want to see her again.

"I love you, Marli," Dad said quietly. "What I'm also trying to say is that I want another chance . . . a chance to be a good father to you and Kyle."

Marli sat back down on the bed. Some of her anger was melting. She touched his hand. "I love you, too, Dad."

"Thanks, Marli Lou. But before you go, there's just one more thing—"

Marli perked up. "What is it?"

"I told Kyle already. I asked him to keep it quiet because I wanted to tell you myself."

"Say what's on your mind," Marli prodded.

Dad flashed a grin. "You've got a little sister."

Marli felt a jolt. "What do you mean?"

"I got married again a few years ago," Dad explained in a rush. "She's three and a half, and her name is Meredith. For short, we call her Meri."

Marli glared. *"We?"*

"My second wife, Gail, and I," Dad said sheepishly. "I can't wait to take my three kids out together."

Marli got up and backed toward the door. "You're too much, Dad," she said accusingly, struggling to keep her voice down. "You're nuts, dropping something like that on me and Kyle out of the blue."

She fumbled for the doorknob. "Good luck on your heart operation."

Outside in the corridor, Marli saw Ma chatting with Aunt Dee Dee. Kyle was standing close to the door, sipping a cup of hot chocolate.

"Did Dad tell you? Isn't it great?"

"I wouldn't say it was great to keep your second marriage a secret from your own children," Marli sputtered. She wrestled Kyle's chocolate out of his hand and took a swallow.

"Ouch," she yelped. "That's hot."

"That's why it's called *hot* chocolate," Kyle said, taking his drink back. "So, what do you think?"

"I think it's really mean of Dad to leave us in the dark," hissed Marli. "We have a sister we've never met."

"That could be her over there," Kyle whispered. He pointed across the waiting room to a child with lots of braids, wearing a pink dress. The girl was sitting next to a woman who might have been her mother. As Marli and Kyle came closer, they heard her singing.

Meri Lou is falling down,
Falling down, falling down.
Meri Lou is falling down—

"Wow," said Kyle, "isn't that our song?"

Marli shook her head. "Dad must have taught her. Why didn't he tell us about her?"

Kyle shrugged. "Dad's a mysterious dude."

"Oh, well," said Marli begrudgingly, "at least we got to see him."

The woman next to Meredith got up and approached them. "I'm Gail," she said, extending her hand first to Marli and then to Kyle. "I've been hoping to meet you someday."

"Nice meeting you," said Marli, surprised that the woman knew them.

Marli turned to the little girl. "And what's your name?"

The child smiled brightly. She had dimples just like Marli's.

"Meredith," she said politely. Her voice was really cute.

Marli knelt down to her level. "Guess who I am."

She threw her arms around Marli's neck. "You're Marli, my big sister! And that's my brother, Kyle."

Kyle stooped over. "Wow, she knows us!"

"Daddy showed me your picture," said Meredith.

Marli turned away. For the second time that day, tears fell from her eyes. Dad hadn't forgotten her and Kyle after all. He'd even told Meredith about them and shown her their picture. But where had the picture come from? Maybe Aunt Dee Dee had sent it to him; she'd come to visit them one time the year before. . . .

Gail went in to visit Dad, leaving Meredith with

Marli. When Gail left, Ma walked over. Aunt Dee Dee was behind her.

"Leave it to your father," Ma remarked, glancing at Meredith. "The little girl is really sweet, though."

"A child is never a bad thing," said Aunt Dee Dee. After stroking Meredith's hair, she gave Kyle and Marli hugs.

"I'm so glad to see you," Aunt Dee Dee whispered in Marli's ear.

Marli smiled. She had missed her aunt.

"Maybe after all this, we'll get to see each other more," Kyle piped up.

"Sometimes it takes a crisis to bring folks together," said Aunt Dee Dee.

Marli took Meredith's hand and strolled toward the window. "Have you ever seen cherry blossoms?"

Meredith shook her head. "What do they look like?"

Marli lifted her sister up. "Pink and beautiful, just like your dress. And guess what? *Cherry* rhymes with *Meri!*"

The little girl giggled.

"Maybe someday we'll go see them together," said Marli.

"Promise?" said Meredith.

Marli gazed outside. Though Dad was sick, the world looked brighter, because she'd gotten to see him. But after his operation, no telling what would happen. She had so many questions, and deep down she was still angry. But the greatest thing was that she'd met her little sister.

"Promise?" Meredith asked again. "That we can see the blossoms?"

Marli smiled and hugged her closer. "Yes, Meri. I promise."

Happily (Sorta) Ever After (Maybe)

By

Dian Curtis Regan

"Then Mama Worm and Baby Worm wriggled away in the damp soil, happily ever after," reads my brother, Nate, to the giant belly of his expecting wife, Cinta, ballooning next to him on the sofa.

"The end," he adds, winking at me. "Do you like that one, Lexi?"

"Gag me with a baby spoon," I scoff, scrunched onto my third of the sofa—a *sliver* of the sofa, actually. "Who writes this dreck?"

"This was in the box of books Mom sent from Nanjing."

"Oh," I say. "Our *mother* is responsible. Figures."

"Don't start in on Mom again."

My brother shoots me an aggravated look as he flips the book closed. The cover is crawling with smiley-faced baby worms.

"Ewwww. Good thing you're having a boy."

Cinta laughs, and we knuckle bump.

I peel myself off the sofa. I should go upstairs to my broom-closet-of-a-guest-room so Nate and Cinta can have some alone time in their tiny house.

My brother is a law student by day and a grocery clerk by night. Cinta mostly sits on the sofa, miserable with the heat and her hugeness. She worries over lost income from tips, now that she's too close to her due date to waitress.

When Mom first asked Nate if I could stay with them while she was working in China and Dad was stationed overseas, he assured her they had plenty of room. His answer was about as realistic as worms with happy-people faces.

"Oh, wait, Lex," Cinta says. "I have something for you." Dark hair falls across her face as she lists starboard to reach into the side pocket of her maternity top. She pulls out an envelope. "It's an invitation to my baby shower. Saturday at Applebee's."

"Thanks." I take the invitation and go upstairs, thumb-tacking the card onto a Peg-Board. How can I buy a gift for Cinta? Mom left money with Nate to cover the added expense of a houseguest, but I don't want to ask for any of it because I know they need it for more important things, like groceries, rent, and utilities.

The temperature in my room is a thousand degrees on this muggy Kansas afternoon. There's nothing to do except lie on the bed beneath the ceiling fan and try to cool off.

Nate was my age—thirteen—when I was born, and I'll be his age—twenty-six—when my nephew is thirteen. Amazing.

The thought of being an aunt makes me smile. Still, I'd rather await the blessed event from afar—like my own bedroom in my own house an hour away from here. Who knew I'd be living with Nate and Cinta right when the baby is due? I love reading stories with twists and turns, but I do *not* want twists and turns jumping out at me in real life.

Mom was supposed to return from Nanjing before Dad shipped out. But start-up for the plant she's engineering was delayed. I tried everything to get Dad to let me stay home, or—Plan B—move in with my friend Kara until Mom returned.

Things that didn't work: yelling, slamming doors, the silent treatment.

It's tough having a navy captain for a father.

The August sun shoots rays into my eyes as it melts toward the horizon. I sit up and look out the window. A neighbor kid about my age is reading in his yard, hunched on top of a plastic slide.

Maybe a breeze has kicked up by now. I head downstairs to a backyard as tiny as my room. Four steps along a sidewalk gets me to the gate. A picnic table takes up one side of the walk, and the remains of a tiny garden lie dying on the other side.

Cinta was all gung ho about the garden in the spring when she planted it, but by July, she couldn't bend over to weed it. I know it's been hard for her to watch the plants she so carefully nurtured get choked by weeds, then shrivel beneath the relentless sun.

And yes, I know I should offer to salvage what's left of the garden—mostly puny tomatoes—but why cooperate? I want everyone to know I do *not* appreciate being dumped on my brother's family. And don't get me started on the fact that this arrangement is going to totally mess up the beginning of eighth grade for me.

The new girl in a new school with no friends? Oh, joy.

After Mom returns, I can move home and go back to my old school, but by then I'll have missed the fall dance, the games, the Halloween parties, sleepovers, and just hanging out with Kara and the gang.

Who thinks this is a good idea? Not I.

I notice the guy next door is watching me inspect the garden. I move to the picnic table, sitting on top so I can see over the fence separating our yards. The guy on the plastic slide and I are practically sitting side by side.

"Hey," I say. "I'm Lexi."

"Trev," he answers, then holds my gaze as if waiting for an explanation of who I am and why I've suddenly shown up on Hopper Street.

"Nate's my brother," I tell him, pointing toward the house. "My parents are overseas, so I'm staying here till my mom gets home." Just saying the words makes my heart tip over in anger.

The guy closes his book as if my comment, laced with sarcasm, warrants further investigation. "What country?"

"My mom's in China. My dad's on a navy ship in the Persian Gulf."

"Wow," Trev says, looking impressed.

"What do *your* parents do?" I ask.

He hesitates, as though comparing his answer to mine. "My dad works on the space station, and my mom is a spy."

"Seriously?"

He shrugs. "Naw. Your story's better."

I didn't know it was a competition.

"My dad actually works at a bank," he tells me. "My mom homeschools me."

"Oh." Envy wraps my heart in a jealous hug. How normal his life sounds. "What grade are you in?"

"We don't do grades. I progress at my own speed. And I'm fourteen, if that's what you want to know."

I did. "What are you reading?"

He picks up the book and shows me the cover. *The Guinness Book of World Records.* "My mom assigns me lots of fiction, but on my own time, I prefer a book with facts."

"Oh," I say. *Boy genius.* "So, do you know anything about baby worms?"

My question startles him, then he chuckles. "As a matter of fact . . ."

After dinner, it's story time again. *Baby Bunny's Birthday.*

Why do I subject myself to this torture? First, there's nothing else to do in this munchkin house, and second, I miss being home with Mom and Dad. There, I said it.

Tonight's story: Bunny Mama makes bunny cakes for her "bouncy baby bunny's birthday." (Whuh?)

The entertainment value is watching Nate captivate his audience. (Me and Giant Belly.) The other audience member dozed off in the middle of the Baby Bunny Bop.

"Isn't it wrong to lie to kids?" I ask Nate. "I mean, even before your son is born, you're lying to him."

Nate crinkles his forehead, which I know means, *What the heck are you talking about?*

"Bunnies don't speak," I say. "They don't bake cakes, and they don't celebrate birthdays. And worms don't snuggle together in the damp soil. Trev says baby worms aren't even *born*. They hatch from cocoons the size of a grain of rice. They don't bond with their mother, who is *also* their father—which is so weird I don't even want to think about it."

"Trev?"

"The boy next door."

"Oh." Nate nods. "Lighten up, Lex, the stories aren't meant to teach anything; they're just for fun."

"Well, I don't like it. Stories should tell the *truth*."

I think of my parents at that exact moment. Why? I don't know. But I *do* think Mom should have told me there was a huge possibility she wouldn't be home before my father had to leave—or before school started.

And what about the stuff Dad told me? He says he's safe because he's on a massive ship and not near actual fighting. Is that true? Or is it something Bunny Daddy might tell Bunny Baby so everyone feels all warm and fuzzy and safe?

Let's be honest here.

I go upstairs to the oven that is my bedroom. The window is open, but the breeze is as thin as the bunny tale.

I think about other stories I've bought into: Santa Claus, the Big Pond in the Sky where my goldfish Lester went after Mom flushed him. I've even checked the back wall of my closet multiple times, hoping to locate the secret doorway to Narnia. Lies.

Suddenly, I have the urge to read something factual to take my mind off my family's well-intentioned fudging of the truth.

I scan Cinta's bookshelf. Yes, I find nonfiction, but . . . *What to Expect When You're Expecting*? No, thank you. *Your Baby's First Year*? Not interested.

Second shelf: more Chinese baby books.

Mom, you've got to be kidding.

I sit on the bed and read *Baby Elephant Does Ballet.*

OMG, what are we doing to the minds of babies? Born or unborn?

I admit that the sight of an elephant in a tutu is comical, but with all due respect to the author, how does a dancing elephant twist an ankle? Do elephants even *have* ankles? I wonder if Trev can fill me in about elephant ankles the way he did about worms who bat for both teams.

Climbing into bed, I kick off the unneeded covers and think about a gift I could take to the baby shower. An idea hits me and I reach for a notebook. I'll give Cinta a *true and honest* family story to read to her baby bump. With actual people instead of animals saying treacly things.

Once upon a time, I write.

Wait. Not original. I cross it out.

Once, in a town in Kansas . . .

No. Too specific. Besides, when people think of Kansas, they think of that *other* children's tale—the one with the tornado, the witch, and the little dog, too.

I begin again:

Once there was a family. The father worked at a bank. The mother stayed home with the new baby.

A half hour later, that's still all I've written.

Writing a story is hard.

If the father isn't going to wear a tutu and twist his ankle or the mother isn't going to say to the kid, "Call me Mommy *and* Daddy," then I've got a pretty boring story.

Maybe those writers in China *do* know a thing or two about writing for babies.

The next morning, I peer out the kitchen window a zillion times to see if Trev is in his yard. Dumb, I know. But Kara is on vacation with her family, so I don't have anyone to talk to.

Nate has taken Cinta to the doctor for a sonogram. I was invited, but I'd rather stick pins in my eyes than sit in a waiting room with a bunch of mothers and little kids.

I could e-mail Mom on Nate's computer, but I don't want her to think all is well or that her daughter is happy. Besides, it's the middle of the night in Nanjing, which is thirteen hours ahead of Kansas. This prevents us from IM-arguing in real time.

We hear from Dad when he can use one of the computers on the ship. It's all high security, so even if he wants to say, "Hi, Lexi, I miss you," the message is scrutinized for ulterior meanings and might take hours or even days to arrive in my e-mail box.

Yet, I suppose if "Hi, Lexi, I miss you" is intercepted by the enemy and confuses them, then we've done our part to serve our country.

I hear a car pull up. Nate and Cinta come inside. Nate is grinning, and Cinta is wiping tears from her eyes.

"What's wrong?" I say. "My God, what's wrong? The baby . . . ?"

"The babies are fine," Nate says.

"Then why is Cinta—" I stare at my brother. "Did you say *babies*?"

Cinta nods, now laughing and crying at the same time. "Two babies, Lexi. Twins! Two little boys."

"Whoa." I sink onto the sofa as if I'm the one who needs support. Cinta plops next to me. No wonder she's gotten as big as a dancing elephant. Two babies!

"How come you didn't know this earlier?" I ask, confused.

Nate drops his gaze. "In an effort to save money, we agreed to only two sonograms—one early on and one late-term. Apparently, it's possible to miss a second fetus at the beginning."

I know it pains him to bring up the issue of money, since law school is their biggest expense. They scrimped to buy a crib, and now? They'll have to buy two of everything.

"Is there anything I can do?" I ask, feeling awful about bucking the living arrangements and, in general, being difficult. "Why not take the money I'd have to borrow from you to buy a baby shower gift and put it toward whatever you need?"

Nate gives me a hug. "Thank you, Lex."

"And if you need me out of the guest room," I tell him, "I'm perfectly capable of moving home until—"

"No way!"

For one brief second, I'd hoped to win the battle with Nate that I'd lost with Mom and Dad. I've even fantasized about being home alone and getting The Call from a hysterical Cinta on a day when Nate's in school. I'd jump into Mom's car and race to pick up my sister-in-law, then rush her to the hospital.

I'd be everybody's hero.

Okay, so I'm too young to drive. Plus, I don't know how. My fantasy is as unrealistic as bunnies blowing out candles. . . .

I take my lunch outside to eat on the picnic table so Nate and Cinta can have some privacy to discuss the fact that they'll soon be a four-person family living in a matchbox. *Five*-person, if you count "Aunt Lexi."

This is driving me crazy. Is it too late to order another family? One in which Mom and Dad are home and brother graduates from law school, gets a job, *then* gets married? Buys a big house, *then* starts a family?

"Hey, Lexi!"

Trev is leaning over the fence, a Dr Pepper in one hand and a book in the other. *Baseball: Then and Now.*

This guy is definitely a reader—and I'll bet he wasn't brought up on fuzzy-wuzzy wabbit books.

"I've been waiting for you to come outside," he says.

Oooff. I don't mention that *I've* been waiting all morning for *him* to make an appearance.

I offer half my sandwich.

He takes it, grinning.

"Can I ask you a question?" I say.

He nods while taking a bite.

"What sort of fiction did your teacher-mom start you off reading when you were a baby? I mean, did you read talking animal stories?"

Dumb question, but I want to understand how a guy who's obviously smart got that way. I'll have two nephews to take care of soon. I have responsibilities.

He squints at the overcast sky, thinking. "My mom had

me reading from day one—or at least looking at books and chewing on them." He pauses. "I'm sure some of the animals talked. Heck, they still do. Haven't you read *Animal Farm* or *Watership Down*?"

"Um, no." I had no idea animals talked in grown-up books. I wonder if *they* speak the truth?

"When I was nine or ten," Trev adds, "I read encyclopedias. That's why I know so much about worms. It's all there in the W volume."

He punctuates his comment with a goofy expression and makes me laugh. We spend the next hour talking about books and families. I'm amazed by how easy it feels to hang out with him—like a friend, and not like a boy. Who knew?

Tonight, Cinta can barely drag herself to the kitchen to contemplate dinner. I know the multiple-baby news has done her in for the day.

My guilt level over being one more unexpected burden in her life gets the better of me, so I insist on fixing dinner instead of paying for takeout. Cinta is pleased. She goes off to take a nap while I fix mac and cheese, adding tuna and peas in an attempt to make it healthier.

Outside, I pick the last of the puny tomatoes and pull up three carrots. I even find a few baby cucumbers hiding beneath leaves—enough veggies to make a salad.

I find a tablecloth in a hutch that once belonged to my grandmother, then pop five backyard daisies into a glass of water for a centerpiece.

When my brother arrives home, he's *so* impressed that his little sister has committed cooking (if that's what you call it), he tells me I can live in the guest room forever.

I fail to find this amusing.

After dinner, we stay at the table and make a long-distance call to Nanjing, hoping to catch Mom at the hotel before she goes off into her day. Telling her she'll be having *two* grandsons instead of one is definitely news to be delivered "in person," not via e-mail.

Nate breaks the news. I can hear Mom's surprise and delight from five feet away.

He puts Cinta on the phone. As I listen to her answer questions, mixed emotions stir my guilt again. I really *want* to stay angry at my mother, but . . .

Cinta hands me the phone.

"Hi, sweetie," Mom says.

When I hear her voice, I start to cry. I don't know why; I must be PMSing.

"It's okay, Lexi," Mom says. "Isn't it wonderful? You're going to be the aunt of two nephews!"

I nod, which is stupid because she can't see me. I feel like an idiot for blubbering on the phone. "I miss you, Mom," I say.

"I miss you, too. I'm sorry I won't be finished here until after the boys are born. The boys!" she repeats, sounding thrilled. "My darling twin grandsons!"

Then Mom adds, "I'll be home soon, Lexi."

I'm starting to hate the word *soon*. Give me an exact date, please. Stick to the facts.

I hand the phone back to Nate so I can find some tissues. He's smirking at me. I'm sure he finds it amusing that one "Hi, sweetie" from our mother is enough to melt my anger.

I pretend to smack him.

We want to call Dad, too, but that call is trickier. We pretty much have to wait for him to call us when he can. Still, we gather around Nate's computer and help him compose a GUESS WHAT? e-mail to "Grandpa."

At tonight's story time, I suffer mightily.

But I'm a good aunt, so I've taken my spot on the sofa to monitor the mental junk food my nephews are being exposed to.

Will Baby Monkey *ever* find the friggin' banana tree where Mommy Monkey ordered him to wait for her? I am *so* relieved when the clueless chimp spots those stupid green bananas on the horizon, monkey-lopes up the hill, then flings himself into Mommy's furry arms.

Do monkeys really do such things? I think not.

Lies, all lies!

"May I read next?" I ask, grabbing a book I stashed earlier behind the sofa.

"What are you doing with my old high school encyclopedias?" Nate asks. "We should give those away; they're taking up valuable space in the storage room. Besides, Google is all anyone needs nowadays."

"I disagree, big brother."

Scooching closer to Giant Belly on my sliver of the sofa, I open the A volume and speak directly to the multiple baby bump. "Listen up, my nameless nephews, tonight we shall begin reading true and honest stuff."

Nate rolls his eyes and slides in on Cinta's other side. "This is just a phase she's going through," he whispers, loud enough for me to hear. "Teenagers! It will pass."

Ignoring him, I dive in. "We begin, boys, with *aardvark*. An aardvark is a nocturnal animal from Africa. It also goes by the names *ant bear, anteater, earth hog,* or *earth pig.* Its teeth wear down from constant burrowing and are continuously replaced."

"Wow, permanent teeth replacement," Cinta says, perking up. "How handy would *that* be?" She pats her belly. "Pay attention, sons. We could all learn a thing or two from Aunt Lexi. . . ."

Later, in bed beneath the ceiling fan, with the window wide open, I think about Cinta's comment, and it puffs me up with pride.

I don't know what it was about that exact moment on the sofa with Nate and Cinta and the babies, but it felt important.

Tonight was the first time I didn't feel like the little girl who has to be taken care of while her parents are away. The Baby Monkey who can't stay home alone.

I felt listened to. I felt like a grown-up part of my family.

And, okay, having a conversation with a boy today without getting tongue-tied with embarrassment certainly helped.

Getting out of bed, I take a phone book from Cinta's shelf and look up the location of the nearest library. Tomorrow, I'll browse their nonfiction picture books for new Giant Belly reading choices. Maybe Trev will tag along to the library with me.

I climb back into bed and think about my family. Near or far, they may drive me crazy, but still, we take care of each other. We do.

And that's a *fact*.

By

Joan Bauer

"It's going to be a lovely wedding, if it *kills* me," my mother snarled. "And it just might *because* . . ." She took a deep breath; her eyes looked wild.

I braced myself for the seating drama.

"We can't sit Uncle Bud next to Emerald because Emerald has three cats and Uncle Bud is allergic to cats and just being near Emerald makes his throat close up! We can't sit him next to Charles because Charles whines and it makes Bud crazy."

"Why don't you put him next to Aunt Irma, Mom?"

Mom closed her eyes. "Because of the funeral."

When Uncle Bud's mother died, she was buried wearing the necklace Irma always wanted.

"Can't they just get over it?" I asked.

My mother put her head in her hands. "Yes, Gracie, in a perfect world, they could." She looked miserably at the seating chart for my big sister Hannah's upcoming wedding. One hundred and twenty-three people were coming, half of whom couldn't sit next to each other.

"I could just elope," Hannah shouted from the next room.

"We've already put down the deposit for the reception," Mom said icily.

Hannah poked her head in the kitchen. "Gracie, you are the family diplomat. I'm counting on you to keep the peace."

My mother nodded hopefully. I'd won three awards for diplomacy for my high school's Model UN team. Model UN is an academic competition that simulates the real United Nations.

I smiled nervously.

"Promise me you'll do this." Hannah's face looked tight.

"I'll try, but I'm really more effective with international crises, and—"

"Promise me!"

I gulped. "I promise."

Hannah clenched her jaw. "And, remember, we can't put Brad's mother next to his brother because she's a conservative and his brother is a liberal and they fought all through Lonnie's wedding."

Mom looked at the seating chart again. "We could put the conservatives near the band. The liberals could sit at the two long tables near the ice sculpture swans, and the moderates could sit between them." She sighed. "Maybe we could make up red state tables and blue state tables—"

"My colors," Hannah yelped, *"are blush and rose!"*

"There's still time to move to red and blue," I mentioned.

Hannah's perfectly waxed eyebrows furrowed. "Gracie"— her voice was low and threatening—"could I speak to you *alone?*"

My sister took my arm and yanked me into the living room. We stood by the fireplace under the big, grinning extended family photo taken at my cousin Lonnie's wedding that was, and I'm not being overly dramatic here, a test from God that my family flunked.

"Mom won't listen, Gracie, so I'm telling you. I am hurt to the core that most of my bridesmaids have refused to buy the sequined shoes that were featured in all the major bride magazines!"

I was one of the bridesmaids and decided not to mention that the shoes cost a fortune.

"They're the *now* shoes, Gracie. The *it* shoes." She shoved a photo in front of me from *Mega Bride* of beaming bridesmaids in pointy, sequined heels.

I nodded.

"I'm getting married in forty-six hours, and everything is going wrong!" Hannah threw down the magazine.

Hannah had been throwing things down a lot this week.

I said, "That's got to feel bad," and stood there.

Hannah bit her quivering lip. "It's been a terrible week. Just terrible."

I knew for a fact that her maid of honor had called her Bridezilla to her face.

"It will all work out," I assured her. "Weddings are complicated."

I handed her a tissue. She blew her nose. "I just want

one day in my life to be absolutely perfect. Is that too much to ask?"

I glanced at the picture of my extended family at Lonnie's wedding. "Well, actually . . ."

Thankfully, Mom shrieked from the kitchen: *"Gracie, where will I put Uncle Moss?"*

I ran back to the kitchen to another desperate woman. I looked at the guest list. "You could put him next to Siegfried."

Mom shook her head. "Moss is a rabid Red Sox fan; Siegfried loves the Yankees."

"People in this family just need to get along!" I insisted.

Hannah stormed in. "And how do you propose we do that?"

"Well, sometimes it's basic things, like just listening to another person, you know; seeing why they feel the way they do!"

Hannah scoffed. "The last time I tried to listen to Uncle Charles complaining about his ex-wives and his health and his anxiety, I got a migraine." Hannah twisted her light brown hair and put it up on her head.

"I like your hair up," Mom said soothingly.

Hannah smiled and twirled around. "Do you think I should braid flowers through my hair or wear the veil?"

"Flowers," I suggested.

"Nonallergenic flowers," Mom warned, "because of Helen, Doris, and Charles. And we have to call the caterer and tell her no walnuts in anything because they make Charles swell up."

"Whose wedding is this?" Hannah snapped.

"Not yours," my fifteen-year-old cousin Gerald said as he walked in through the back door wearing a shirt that read, ACT FIRST—THINK LATER.

Gerald plopped down at the kitchen table.

"How are you, dear?" Mom asked him.

"Ready for world domination," he said. Typical Gerald. He opened his folder from our Model United Nations club. This year our school was going as Luxembourg—not exactly a force on the world stage. Gerald was not pleased.

"I've been thinking, Gracie." He rapped his folder. "Luxembourg needs to declare a war."

I stared at him. "We're a cute, tiny country!"

"With no meaningful geopolitical presence," Gerald said. "We need to show people they can't mess with us."

"No one is trying to mess with us, Gerald!"

"Not yet . . . but I think we have to go to the conference with an edge, you know?"

The big MUN conference was coming up in two weeks. Schools from all over the country were competing. Between that and keeping peace at the wedding, I had more to do than was reasonably, rationally, or emotionally possible.

"I think," my mother said, looking back at the seating chart, "that if I put the Logan sisters at opposite ends of the room—"

"With their backs to each other," Hannah demanded.

"With their backs to each other," Mom acknowledged.

"Because nothing can go wrong on my special day!" Hannah waved a blush and rose cocktail napkin with the words HANNAH AND BRAD FOREVER on it.

"A small war," Gerald said to me earnestly. "Something to get us noticed. People don't think of Luxembourg as a force."

"There's a reason for that, Gerald. We have eight hundred people in our army."

"We can send in the navy."

"Luxembourg is landlocked. We don't have a navy. We need to move diplomatically and"—I sputtered—"I don't need this!"

Gerald grinned. "We could bring out our nukes."

"This is what's wrong with the world! People just think that threats and force are how you get things done."

Hannah shrieked, "And if Lewis and Constance get into it again over their grandfather's inheritance, I swear to you all now, you are witnesses, I'll stand on a table and start screaming and not stop."

Gerald pulled out his research on Luxembourg. "Look, as a country we're rich, we've got major EU influence, we're—"

My cousin Layla was knocking at the door. "Come in," I said. "Gerald is about to declare war."

She walked in nervously. "Uh . . . hi . . ."

"I don't think a war would impact Luxembourg's economy too much," Gerald added.

I smiled at Layla, who said, "Uh . . . hi . . ." again. She's usually a bit more of a conversationalist. "Gracie," she said quietly, "I need to tell you something."

"What?"

Layla looked down. She was the prettiest in the family, with long black hair, perfect skin, and Bambi eyes. It would be easy to hate her if she wasn't so nice.

"You're probably going to hate me, Gracie."

I didn't like the way this was going.

Layla took a huge breath. "Look, it's about Matt."

Matt Dean and I had gone out for seven bittersweet months. I was in love with him—I probably still am, despite the fact that he broke up with me on his blog.

"What about him?" I asked cautiously.

"Okay, look, I know that Matt broke up with you, and I totally don't agree with the way he did it—okay? And it had nothing to do with me because I always told him that while you guys were going out, he could just take a leap if he thought I was going to go out with your boyfriend behind your back."

I started feeling sick to my stomach.

"But Matt and I, well, we're kind of together now."

"You and Matt?" This was hard to process.

"And he wants to come with me to Hannah's wedding. I don't want to hurt you, Gracie." She folded her arms tight across her chest. "But I said okay, he could come. You know how Matt is—persistent." She still hadn't looked at me. "So that's it."

I felt like I'd been punched in the face. "Let me get this straight. You're bringing Matt to Hannah's wedding. . . ."

"Are you okay with this, Gracie?"

"Am I okay that my boyfriend dumped me for my cousin? Or am I okay that your date for the wedding is more important to you than how I feel? Which question do you want me to answer first?"

"I'd take the second one first," Gerald suggested.

"You don't have to be sarcastic!" Layla shouted.

"I think sarcasm is appropriate," Gerald added.

Layla ran out the door.

I stood there looking at the screen door with our little wreath that said A HOME IS NOT A HOME WITHOUT LOVE.

And it's not like I felt like crying—that's not my style. I just felt like I'd been utterly slimed.

I sat down hard. Gerald said, "I move to vote her off the island, Gracie."

"I second that." I closed my eyes.

I *will* be okay.

I'd *better* be okay.

I'm—

"*Not* okay," I heard Hannah shout. She stormed into the kitchen holding her phone to her ear. "You're a florist, right? You deal with flowers that have different colors, right? And you're telling me you *don't have* blush and rose?"

"Gracie . . ." Mom stood at the dining room door. She'd heard.

"Where are you going to seat the fun couple?" I asked bitterly.

Mom looked at the seating chart in her hand. "How 'bout the South Pole?"

I nodded.

"I think we could arrange fourth-class passage to a damp cave in Luxembourg," Gerald added, raising his eyebrows. "I have connections."

I smiled bravely, but my heart wasn't in it.

Mom gave me a hug. "Just remember who you are," she whispered. "That's the first step."

I made myself a list. I am:

Grace Ann Pinter

Age 16

Vice president of Model UN

Winner of three MUN awards for diplomacy

Grade point average—3.8

Student council rep three years running

Decent soccer player

Innovative cook

Good listener

Drop-kicked into the end zone on Matt's blog for the
entire world to see

Mom and I were walking down the street by the park, taking one of the mother-daughter walks where the mother
tries to impart helpful tips for living.

"I think I've figured out who I am," I told her. "What's
the second step?"

Mom laughed. "Look fabulous."

I was feeling utterly unfabulous.

"A key thing to remember, honey. You weren't happy in
that relationship with Matt. Ever."

"Do you think Layla's happy?"

"I don't know."

I met Matt at a Model UN meeting and instantly fell for
him. I was Egypt; he was Syria. All the signs said it couldn't
possibly work—and in the end it didn't. He'd dropped out
of Model UN after we broke up. That was something, I
guess.

How was I going to handle this?

To keep my mind off the wedding, I threw myself into Model UN prep.

"Okay, everybody, listen up." Mr. Dalton, our Model UN adviser, stood before us. "Today we're going to talk about how to achieve consensus in your sessions. Who's got some ideas?"

"Find something that people agree on," I mentioned, "and try to build from there."

"And that could be what?"

Jean Raney raised her hand. "It could be as small as whether they went to the same summer camp or they both like the same kind of food."

Mr. Dalton nodded. "How do you find that out?"

"We listen," I said.

"That's right." He wrote LEARN TO LISTEN on the whiteboard. "You will never build consensus if you don't listen."

Gerald said, "That's not realistic. Countries aren't listening to each other."

"And what does that tell you?" Mr. Dalton asked.

Gerald shrugged. "Listening doesn't work."

"Or"—I stepped in—"we need to get better at it."

Mr. Dalton smiled. "So, my good colleagues of Luxembourg, I challenge you to change the game. Sit down with them and listen."

It was a lovely wedding, really.

And I did look fabulous, if I do say so myself.

The hypoallergenic flowers made a dramatic arch across the front of the church, although Helen, Doris, and Charles had sneezing fits anyway. I only tripped once going down the aisle (I was walking past Layla and Matt as they cooed in the back pew). The aisle was only wide enough for one bride and one and a half parents, so Dad kept stepping on Hannah's gown, which caused Hannah to appear to be lurching toward the altar. But she looked gorgeous, and she made it to the front, where Brad, her groom, was beaming.

Then Hallie, the three-year-old flower girl, announced in the middle of the ceremony that she had to go to the bathroom.

The minister talked about how in every marriage there would be good times and bad times, and several of my relatives poked their spouses.

Uncle Charles cried during the vows, and blew his nose

extra loud, but he was thinking about his three former wives and how they took close to everything he had.

He explained this at the reception, actually. He pulled me over to his table where he was sitting alone. "Sit," he said.

I sat and tried to remember why I'd always liked him.

"Are you still working at that computer company?" I asked him.

"I've worked at three computer companies," Charles groaned. "I'm close to quitting this job."

"I'm sorry it's not working out."

"Well, how could it?" And Charles proceeded to tell me his problems, beginning with how his "so-called coworkers" looked at his computer screen over his shoulder, showed up late for meetings, *never* said please and thank you, chewed gum too loud, talked behind his back, *and* insisted that he had a condescending attitude toward everyone.

"You do have a condescending attitude, Charles." It was Uncle Bud.

Charles's face turned blush and rose. He glared at Uncle Bud. "What did you say?"

Uncle Bud shrugged and sat down.

"What did you just say?" Charles demanded.

Uncle Bud looked at Charles. "You can quit the job, but don't kid yourself. The problems are going to follow you, Charles, no matter how many new jobs you get. You've got to look at yourself and what you bring to the party."

I smiled and said, "This might not be the best time to—"

Charles rose in fury. *"Oh, really?"*

I caught Hannah's extreme bridal gaze across the very crowded room.

Charles's eyes were steely cold as he glared at Bud. "I resent that!"

"I know you do," Bud answered, calmly eating a roll.

Just then Matt and Layla walked by, hand in hand, still cooing. Now I felt like crying.

"What's the matter with you?" Charles demanded.

I bit my lip. "Nothing."

"Who's that guy dancing with Layla?" Bud asked. "I don't like his face."

I told them.

"He dumped you and now he's here with Layla?" Charles said.

"Yeah."

"That's terrible. That's worse than what my first ex-wife did."

"Now, she was a terror," Bud agreed.

"I still have nightmares," Charles added.

"It's good she dumped you," Bud went on, "because nobody liked her."

"Nobody likes me," Charles muttered.

I looked at his sad face and suddenly remembered. "I like you, Charles. I've always liked you. You helped me that time I broke my ankle in first grade. You took me to the hospital and waited there until Mom got back in town. You were terrific."

Charles smiled. "That was a long time ago."

We watched Layla and Matt on the dance floor, dancing just this side of dirty.

"He's got something sleazy about him," Bud said. "You're well rid of him. But, look, I got dumped bad once, and I fell hard. I can appreciate this isn't your best day."

"Thanks."

"When it happened to me," Bud continued, "I was like the walking wounded. But right after that I met Myrna, and we've been married for thirty-seven years."

Charles looked impressed. "Putting all my marriages together, I wasn't married that long."

We all watched Matt kiss Layla on the nose.

Bud leaned across the table. "Well, let me tell you something, Charles. You and I have had our differences, but Myrna always wanted to set you up with her cousin."

"Which one?"

"The cute one."

Charles leaned forward. "Really?"

"She's over in the corner. I'll introduce you." He hit Charles on the shoulder and called him an old son of a gun. Aunt Irma scowled and brushed against Bud.

"Nice necklace," Bud said to her.

"It could be nicer!" she spat. The funeral issue will never die.

I sat at the table alone as the Logan sisters walked by arguing about how their cat had been cremated.

I sat there listening as Uncle Moss held forth on why America should have a king.

Then I heard, "Gracie, are you mad at me?"

I knew that voice. It was Matt.

I didn't face him. "I don't think we should be talking about this."

"Because it was wrong what I did."

"Well." I tried laughing. "It sure helped make things clear."

"Is this guy bothering you?" It was Uncle Bud with Uncle Charles at his side.

"We were just talking," Matt said.

Uncle Bud turned to Matt. "I hear you've been a pretty busy guy."

"What do you mean?"

"Do I need to spell it out?"

Matt looked at me. "I guess you've been telling everybody."

"She told her *family,*" Charles sneered.

I should have been mortified, but it was really quite nice. And when Charles hissed, "We don't like you," at Matt, well, I just grinned at Matt until he walked away.

"And knock off the dirty dancing," Uncle Bud shouted after him. Then he put one arm around me and one around Charles.

We'd found consensus—getting dumped. Like Mr. Dalton said, you just never know what will bring people together.

Hannah walked over, glistening with bridal joy. "It's so

good to see everyone having a wonderful time. I can't tell you what this means to me."

"Savor it, kid," said Bud, and he headed off to tell Moss exactly what he thought regarding "all this garbage about America getting a king."

It was great practice for the Model UN conference. And when Gerald and I got to the first General Assembly session, we brought Luxembourg into the seat of power.

"So what are you about?" a snide representative from Russia asked me.

"Goodwill," I said.

In all our committees we tried to bring goodwill and a listening ear. We sat down with America and France and got them to agree on agricultural imports. We sat down with four Middle East countries and got some notable consensus on peace. We even coordinated a food bank in a flood-ravaged area in China. Only at the Model UN can you change the world in a weekend.

We didn't win an award that year, but we won something more important—respect.

On the train ride home, Gerald said, "There should be a

trophy for respect, Gracie. A big one like they give at the US Open." He held out his hands like he was receiving it. "I want to thank all the little people who made this possible." He took a bow.

I curled up in my seat and closed my eyes.

"Today, the world," Gerald said. "Tomorrow"—he groaned—"the family."

Midnight Bus to Georgia

By

Walter Dean Myers

The only person you have probably heard of in the Curry family is my cousin Benny. Benny was banned from the East Harlem Pigeon Racing league for giving his fastest pigeon, Lord Tweety, steroids. But that's another story altogether. This is the story of Grandpa Lee Curry, and how we tried to aid and abet him to cross state lines to avoid legal prosecution in the State of New York.

Okay, so I guess you have to know that the Curry family has occasionally done things that some people might shake their heads at. We have two sayings in our family. The first is to do what you got to do to make a dollar, which makes sense to me. The second is to do what you got to do to get out of a bad situation. And what Grandpa Lee had got himself into was definitely a bad situation.

It began (or at least this situation began) when Grandpa Lee read an article in the *Atlanta Journal* saying that the rich paid less taxes than the poor even though they made more money.

"It's taxes that keep the poor man down!" he said.

Being just sixteen, I didn't have a regular job and didn't pay taxes, but I could understand the truth about what Grandpa Lee was saying. So it wasn't really a surprise when he started looking for a way to make money by not paying taxes. Grandpa Lee was not a rash man, nor was he what you would call a lucky man. In his sixty-four years of living on this earth, he had come across a number of likely schemes to get rich, some of which had put him behind bars. In fact, he had been in jail three times, for a total of fourteen years, which was not the hallmark of a lucky man. What Grandpa Lee realized was that if he worked for somebody else, they would take out taxes from his pay and send them right on to the Internal Revenue Service. He needed to be working for himself so that he could decide what he would send, if anything, to pay in taxes. Grandpa Lee and his girlfriend, the fair Imogene, decided to deal in roots and curses. That is, if somebody had a grudge against you and burned roots to bring you bad luck, or put a curse on you in any way, you could go to Grandpa Lee and Imogene and they would get that bad luck or that curse off you. For a fee, of course.

Since many people in DeKalb County, Georgia, were down on their luck and were pretty much convinced that somebody had put a curse on them, business was pretty good from the start. But then one day the police came to Grandpa Lee's house and said that a complaint had been lodged against him.

It seemed that a woman had come to Grandpa Lee and told him that her husband had convinced her to sell their house so that they could retire to Florida. But instead of retiring with her, he took half the money and ran off with another woman. Since that fateful day, she had had nothing but bad luck, headaches, and pains in her left knee, which she took to mean that her husband had not only run off but put a curse on her while he was doing it.

Grandpa Lee had explained to the woman that the husband, obviously a low-life scoundrel, had not only put a curse on her, which caused her headaches, but he had also put a curse on the woman's half of the money. Her very life, he explained, was in danger. He then proceeded to save her life by relieving her of the cursed money.

"She was truly blessed to find me in the nick of time." That is what Grandpa Lee told the cops. The police were somewhat skeptical of Grandpa Lee. But when the police also found a .38 caliber pistol in one shoe box and a number of empty wallets in another, they not only gave him the fish eye but, despite his protests, handcuffed him like a common criminal and hauled him off to jail. He had a hearing at the courthouse the next day, at which time the assistant district attorney accused him of being a con man and a thief. His bail was set at ten thousand dollars, but Grandpa Lee told the judge that his wife had suffered a heart attack and he needed to go up to the medical center in Boston to be by her side until they had decided whether or not she needed a transplant.

"They should know by Monday, Your Honor," he pleaded.

The judge gave him a break and let him go for five days on his own cognizance if he could come up with two character references. The two references Grandpa Lee gave to the court clerk were his brother in Biloxi, Mississippi, and his daughter, my Aunt Nancy, in New York.

Grandpa Lee thanked the judge for his mercy and promised to show up on time, and he and the fair Imogene went right down to the bus station. He sent Imogene up to Roxbury in Boston to stay with her sister awhile, and he came up to visit us in Harlem.

Everything seemed to be working out just fine with Grandpa Lee living with us and sleeping on the couch until he got arrested on 125th Street and St. Nicholas Avenue for driving a car that didn't exactly belong to him.

"The automobile had a FOR SALE sign on it, and the keys were in the ignition," Grandpa Lee explained to the judge. "I was just trying the car out to see if I wanted to make an offer. If I'd known it had a broken taillight and the officer was going to pull me over, I would have known that I didn't want to buy the piece of junk in the first place!"

Okay, so now you have the background to the story. Grandpa Lee was wanted in Georgia for fraud, for possession of an illegal firearm, for theft (although I thought they were just guessing about the wallets), and for possible foul play in the disappearance of Imogene, who he had called and told to stay up in Boston. He was facing some big time in Georgia. That state hands out years like they are jelly beans and they want everybody to have a good time.

Now, the beauty of America is that it is a big country. It's bigger than most people think it is. So it wasn't a surprise when we found out that the police in New York didn't know right away that Grandpa Lee was wanted in Georgia. What we needed to do was to get him out of jail and out of New York and up to Boston where he and Imogene could once again find happiness.

Did I tell you I lived with my Uncle Jimmy and Aunt Nancy? I do. There are stories that my father fell off a ship and drowned when he was in the navy and that my mother was a traveling lady, whatever that means. I don't remember either of them too clearly, but I love Uncle Jimmy and Aunt Nancy with all my heart and thank them for raising me so well.

The first thing we had to do was to bail Grandpa Lee out of jail, which is not easy when you know that he is not going to show up for his court date. We went down to that legal defense outfit you see on television after two in the morning and met up with a young lawyer with pimples and a lot of hope that Everything Would Turn Out All Right. He went to the courthouse and talked to the district attorney's office and pleaded his case. His case was that the only thing that Grandpa Lee wanted to do was to go back to his beloved home in Georgia. Aunt Nancy, the sweetest woman you ever met, showed the assistant district attorney the ticket she had bought for Grandpa Lee to go home and even shed a tear as she told the woman how she was going to miss him.

The point was that New York City has as many cases as they will ever need and then some. If Grandpa Lee went back to Georgia, they wouldn't have to bother with his case in New York and that was just fine with them.

The assistant district attorney went for it and let Grandpa Lee go free on condition that he stay out of trouble and leave the state within twenty-four hours. Aunt Nancy signed the papers releasing Grandpa Lee, saying she would see to it that he got on the midnight bus to Georgia. Everything was good, except for the fact that Grandpa Lee was so tickled about how smooth everything had gone down, he didn't want to leave New York. That's when we found out that Grandpa Lee had some legal expertise, too.

"The only serious cases they got against me in Georgia," he said, the stogie he was chewing on bobbing up and down in the corner of his mouth, "is failing to appear at the hearing, illegal firearms, and the little business about those wallets. That woman believed her money was cursed, and she insisted I take it from her, and she, being a churchgoing woman, will have to admit that. That fraud stuff came to her later when she got to telling her friends about it.

"Now, considering them first three charges from DeKalb County, I ain't really worried about none of them because they can't prove I didn't just find those wallets, and that gun wasn't concealed none, and they got to give me the benefit of the doubt unless they bring Imogene back to Georgia and she gets to talking about how we planned to get our hands on that woman's money. But I can take care of that, too."

"I don't think you should kill Imogene," Uncle Jimmy said. "That don't look good."

"I'm not going to kill her," Grandpa Lee said. "I'm going to marry her and make her my wife. In Georgia they cannot make a woman testify against her legal husband. Since she is the only witness to the plans, that lets me go free and clear!"

That was a good idea, but it brought up another problem.

"We need to have us a family conference," Aunt Nancy said after Grandpa Lee had put on his new silk suit and went out to the bar. "If Grandpa gets picked up by the police again before he goes back to Georgia, they might start charging us with obstruction of justice and anything else they can throw at us."

"So what do we have to do?" Uncle Jimmy asked.

"Get him married to Imogene right away so that he won't mind going back to Georgia," Aunt Nancy said, "and then get him on the bus before he gets all of us into trouble."

We all said a hearty amen to that idea because it was getting clear that Grandpa Lee was a little more than we could handle.

That evening Aunt Nancy called Boston and spoke to Imogene and told her that she had to get right down to New York and marry Grandpa Lee as soon as she could.

"It is a matter of urgent importance," Aunt Nancy said.

"What about Harry?" Imogene asked.

"Who is Harry?" Aunt Nancy asked.

"He is my husband who disappeared on a rainy night in Memphis fifteen years ago," Imogene said.

"Are you kidding me?" Aunt Nancy asked. "Does Lee know you were married?"

"I think he does," Imogene answered. "He helped me to sell those old guitars Harry had around the house. We got over two hundred dollars for them, but I can't get married again as long as I don't know exactly what happened to my first husband. It just ain't right. I hope he didn't find somebody else."

To some families, this would have been a disaster, but not to the Curry family. Aunt Nancy had two kinds of part-time jobs. She dabbled a little in real estate, and she also dabbled a little in arranging marriages. Real estate was hot, and she was pretty good at that, even though it was just a summer job. What she did was to find abandoned buildings and rent out rooms in them. The buildings were usually in pretty bad shape, but she didn't charge much for them, and since she didn't own them, her expenses weren't too high. Some people might have seen this as illegal, but Aunt Nancy saw the money she earned as her due for all the bother she had to put up with when her clients didn't pay the rent.

"It's not like you can just take them to court, you know," she said.

The other thing that Aunt Nancy did was to marry off American citizens to illegal aliens looking to get their green card. The green card is the one you get that says that you are a legal immigrant. For five hundred dollars, Aunt Nancy would find the alien a wife or a husband and arrange a marriage. For a thousand dollars, she would find somebody who spoke a little of whatever language the illegal was speaking so they could say hello to them if they had a mind to. Sometimes she just arranged marriages between Americans who couldn't find husbands or wives of their own. That only cost three hundred dollars.

"If Imogene is afraid to get married, we'll just have to find us a stand-in," Aunt Nancy said.

So what she came up with for Grandpa Lee was to find a girl who was going to stand in for Imogene and marry Grandpa Lee. Then, if the courts down in Georgia ever tried to get Imogene to testify against him, his lawyer could challenge it.

When Grandpa Lee got home, he was as drunk as a skunk, and so we had to wait until the next day to give him the good news.

"I am surprised to find out that Imogene is married," he said. "I thought she was just slow in getting around to it."

Aunt Nancy agreed that the confusion was probably Imogene's fault and went on to explain her idea of having a marriage ceremony with a stand-in bride. Grandpa Lee liked that idea a lot.

"I can be married to her and not married to her at the same time," he said. "There's some genius in what you talking about. Sheer genius."

Everything seemed simple enough, but it wasn't going to stay that way. The woman that Aunt Nancy got to stand in for Imogene was an exchange student from Africa she had been dealing with for a while. When I first saw Samantha Imafidon from Cameroon, I really liked her. She was eighteen and as pretty as she wanted to be. What I didn't like about her was that she was smart. She was a freshman in college and I still had a year to go before I was eligible to take the GED. But, being poor from Africa and everything, she always needed money, so Aunt Nancy had married her off about four or five times whenever she needed a stand-in bride.

The complications set in when Grandpa Lee laid his eyes on Samantha. Okay, I said she was pretty. The truth was that Samantha was an absolute beauty, and that little Cameroon accent she had could just knock you out cold. Put those looks together with that accent and wrap them all up in her big, dark eyes and what you get is Grandpa Lee's heart beating hard enough to jump out his chest.

"You can't marry her as Samantha," Aunt Nancy said. "You have got to marry her as Imogene so they can't prosecute your butt down in Georgia."

Grandpa Lee wasn't hearing none of it.

"Nancy," he said with this real serious look on his face, "for the first time in my life I am in love. You have got to help me marry Samantha on the up-and-up because we are family and we need as much love in this family as we can get."

Okay, so here we go. Grandpa Lee needed to be married to Imogene so he wouldn't be put in jail in Georgia. We needed him to be married to Imogene so he would leave Harlem. But Grandpa Lee had fallen in love with Samantha and wanted to trick her into becoming his permanent wife. Samantha needed the money Aunt Nancy was paying her to stand in for Imogene. Imogene needed to know what happened to Harry.

Did I tell you that Aunt Nancy was a fast thinker? She was. She got right on the phone and called Imogene in Roxbury and told her she had to have a case marriage. Naturally Imogene asked her what a case marriage was.

"That's a marriage you have in case Harry is dead and

his soul is grieving because you are alone and lonely," Aunt Nancy said. "If he ain't dead, then the marriage don't count. And we can have the marriage right over the phone with you up in Roxbury so that will give Harry more time to show up in case he ain't dead."

Imogene could see that and agreed to having a wedding over the phone.

What she decided to do was to have a double wedding. She was going to have Imogene on the telephone and Samantha in the living room.

Aunt Nancy had already told Samantha that she wasn't getting married for real and there was nothing to worry about.

"But after the marriage and she's about ready to go home alone," Grandpa Lee folded his hands in front of his chest as he spoke, "I'll spring the magnificent news on her that our marriage is legit and she will be mine until death doth us part!"

"I'm sure she'll be delighted," Aunt Nancy said, rolling her eyes toward the ceiling.

It was Aunt Nancy's first double wedding in a long time, but she pulled it off. Mr. Liburd from the corner cleaners came through with a wedding dress that was being cleaned for some rich white folks downtown whose ceremony wasn't until the following weekend.

The wedding and community breakfast (four dollars for two eggs, or six dollars if you wanted sausages) was held at the Milbank Recreational Center, which was closed for repairs (Aunt Nancy had somehow acquired the keys), bright and early on Sunday morning. Reverend Fairwell Fletcher conducted the ceremony with the Holy Bible in his right hand and a cell phone in his left on which he had called Imogene. To me it was absolutely beautiful. But nothing comes without a hitch, and the first hitch came about a half hour after the wedding.

Uncle Jimmy had a company, which he called 18K. He would buy nine-karat gold rings, bracelets, and necklaces for twenty-five dollars a pound direct from a store in Chinatown. Then we had a stamp with our store name that we could hit with a hammer and imprint right on that jewelry. So everything we sold read 18K on the inside.

Uncle Jimmy and Aunt Nancy were in the back room selling the jewelry when they heard a commotion coming from the front room. It turned out that Grandpa Lee wanted to take Samantha off on a romantic honeymoon to the sunny South Bronx right then and there. Samantha was trying to fight him off, and Mr. Liburd was trying to get his wedding dress off of her before she tore it up so he could get it cleaned up for the white folks' wedding.

By the time Aunt Nancy got out front, Samantha was half out of the dress and throwing punches at Grandpa Lee.

"I love me a girl with some fight in her!" Grandpa Lee was saying.

It took me, Uncle Jimmy, and the preacher to get Grandpa Lee calmed. Well, we didn't get him relaxed exactly, but we held him down long enough for Samantha to get dressed in her regular clothes and get out the side door.

Aunt Nancy and Uncle Jimmy found that they barely broke even on the community breakfast and jewelry sale because Samantha had let the wedding dress get torn and Mr. Liburd demanded ten more dollars to get it repaired.

Still, much had been accomplished. Grandpa Lee did sort of marry Imogene so she couldn't testify against him down in Georgia and so that was looking good. What was not looking good was Grandpa Lee, laying on the sofa in the living room and letting out the most pitiful wail you ever heard. The truth came down on us like a sudden summer storm. Grandpa

Lee was really in love. Not just your average Grandpa-loves-a-fine-young-chicky love, either. He couldn't sleep. He didn't want anything to drink. He wouldn't even put his false teeth in, just let them sit in a glass on the dresser.

A week later the situation got worse, much worse. The phone rang and Uncle Jimmy answered it. It was a collect call for Grandpa Lee.

"Does it sound like a bill collector?" Aunt Nancy asked. "Lee doesn't have any money."

"I got to answer the phone," Grandpa Lee said. "Maybe Samantha has come to her senses. Maybe she saw the pictures of that white girl getting married wearing the same dress she was married in, and it touched her heart. Or maybe it's my beloved Imogene calling to console me in my hour of grief!"

Reluctantly, Uncle Jimmy handed Grandpa Lee the phone.

"Who? I don't recognize your voice!" Grandpa Lee was saying. "DeKalb County Court? Georgia? What you want? No, this ain't me!"

Well, that shook up Aunt Nancy quite a bit and Uncle Jimmy as well. It didn't have much effect on Grandpa Lee. He was still as lovesick as ever and moaning like a dying calf in a thunderstorm.

But since they had found Grandpa Lee in our house, it didn't look good. Aunt Nancy glanced toward Uncle Jimmy, and Uncle Jimmy rolled his eyes to the ceiling. If the Georgia police knew that Grandpa Lee was at the house, all they had to do was to make a phone call to the New York Police Department to make things ugly in a hurry.

Uncle Jimmy did not want the New York police coming to our house. Over the years he and Aunt Nancy had collected a number of trinkets, including two refrigerators, several microwaves, and a deck of credit cards, that might have given the New York police some small reason to be suspicious of his activities.

"Daddy." Aunt Nancy sat down with her father and looked him dead in the eye. "I think you need a drink to calm your nerves!"

"That I do," Grandpa Lee said.

The first drink they poured for Grandpa Lee filled half a water glass.

"I think Samantha really loves you, but she is afraid to show her true feelings," Aunt Nancy said, pouring a second drink.

"You do?" Grandpa Lee asked.

"She told me that the idea of curling up next to you on a cold winter night was just too thrilling for her to think about," Aunt Nancy went on.

"Too thrilling? Oh, me." Grandpa Lee shook his head.

The second drink was as big as the first one, and Aunt Nancy said that she was going to take Grandpa Lee over to where Samantha lived.

"Take these pills so your breath won't smell bad," she said, giving him two green and pink capsules. "And put your teeth in."

Grandpa Lee got up from the couch, took his teeth from the glass, shook them to get the peroxide off, and slapped them into his mouth. He looked a little woozy by the time we got him dressed, but the next two drinks seemed to help.

"Why am I taking my suitcase?" he asked Aunt Nancy.

Only it came out more like "Why ish I takin' my shoot cashe?"

"So you can start off on your honeymoon right away," Aunt Nancy said. "Have you ever been to Jamaica?"

Okay, so you got the picture. Grandpa Lee was halfway between falling over drunk and standing up and singing drunk by the time we got him to the subway. By the time we got him down to the Port Authority Bus Terminal on Forty-first Street, he had slipped right past roaring drunk into snoring drunk. Uncle Jimmy gave a redcap he knew fifteen dollars to get Grandpa Lee on the midnight bus to Georgia. Then we called Imogene and told her that he was on his way home and for her to get right down to Georgia because he was missing her loving arms something terrible.

And that, more or less, is the story of Grandpa Lee Curry, his adventures in Georgia and Harlem, his falling in love for the first time, and the double wedding and community breakfast.

Me, Aunt Nancy, and Uncle Jimmy had just got home when the police arrived looking for Grandpa Lee. The Georgia police had called the New York police, and the locals had sent two detectives to arrest him for the business in Georgia and for the little matter with the stolen car.

"He was here, but he left to go to Canada," Aunt Nancy said, true to the family honor.

One of the detectives called down to the precinct to see if there were any outstanding warrants on Uncle Jimmy and when he found there weren't any, he said he would be keeping an eye on him anyway.

The end of the story is that Grandpa Lee arrived in Atlanta and was picked up by the local police, who had received a mysterious phone call from New York saying which bus he was going to arrive on. The reward wasn't much, only fifty dollars, and I didn't feel like I had to share it with anybody because they weren't going to let me share in any of the money from the jewelry sale. Fair is fair, the way I see it. Maybe I'll add that to the family sayings.